# The Shropshire Stalker

# THE SHROPSHIRE STALKER

## NICK JONES

YOUCAXTON PUBLICATIONS

OXFORD & SHREWSBURY

# Contents

## Acknowledgements

The author wishes to thank the following for their assistance with the research for this book: Chris Lipscombe of RedEye Marketing; Ludlow Bookbinders; Ludlow Historical Research Group; court officials of Shrewsbury Crown Court; and West Mercia Police. Special thanks also to my dear friend Sasha Lubetkin, for her meticulous proof-reading; to Ant Barroclough for computer advice; and to Bob Fowke of publishers YouCaxton, for his painstaking mentoring throughout the production process.

## Disclaimer

HELL HATH NO FURY LIKE A WOMAN SCORNED
WILLIAM CONGREVE
*THE MOURNING BRIDE* (1697)

# 1

## *Meeting*

BATHED IN SUMMER sunshine and framed by a long avenue of stately conifers, the imposing elevations of Codrington Manor shimmered through the sun-dappled leaves. Small puffy cumuli clouds basked in a cerulean blue sky. Beneath the leafy canopy, an arrow-straight gravel driveway led up to the huge wrought iron gates of the 17th century mansion.

Reflecting the wealth of successive generations of the Codrington dynasty, the three-storey building's steeply-pitched roofs were clad in a mixture of ochre red and lavender hand-made tiles, punctuated by a series of attic gables. Five octagonal brick chimney stacks soared above. Matching two-storey side wings, from a later period, completed the pleasing symmetrical composition, with square, dressed limestone bays enclosing sets of diamond-leaded casement windows.

Beyond the stone piers of the gateway, surmounted by shield-bearing griffons, a broad flagstone path lined by huge banks of lavender led to the manor's ornate timber porch, supported by fluted wooden Tuscan columns.

A low-slung, open-topped silver sports car approached at speed, with the driver's white neckerchief flapping over the rounded cowl of a small leather headrest. The engine's rasping crackle, as it decelerated close to the locked gates, was like an angry hornet and reverberated off the walls of the stately mansion. The car's registration plate showed EVA 55.

Suddenly, its four wheels locked, creating a huge orange dust cloud. With great agility, the driver flipped the steering wheel hard to the left, causing the car to slew sideways, before it finally came to rest only a few feet from the manor gates.

Slowly the dust storm abated, revealing the aerodynamic profile of a vintage Porsche sports-racing car, with a petite woman driver sitting clutching the steering wheel.

She smiled with satisfaction and looked up at a huge canvas banner which was stretched above her head on two wooden poles, marking the entrance to a mown field. In the field were more than 100 cars, all parked in neat rows. The banner read: "PEEL OF BELLS SUMMER FETE – FREE CAR PARK". At either end of the banner were outlines of sets of church bells. Beneath this hoarding – and only inches away from the bonnet of the stationary sports car – a bemused white-coated parking attendant stood frozen to the spot.

Driver and attendant eyed each other suspiciously for several moments. Then as the last of the orange dust settled on the car's bonnet, its woman driver raised herself up from the bucket seat and stood on its squab.

She was wearing the shortest of pleated red tartan mini-skirts over black fishnet stockings. She slowly removed a pair of long silver snakeskin driving gloves and tipped her diamante-studded tortoise shell sunglasses up onto her chestnut-red waved hair. 'Anthony! Fancy nearly running into you!' she called.

The tall, grey-haired custodian of the car park, adjusted his spectacles quizzically and stared intently at the woman. 'Eva? Is it really you?'

'It most certainly is, darling. What a small world!'

'What on earth are you doing in Shropshire?'

Throwing her gloves onto the passenger seat, the diminutive driver grasped the edge of the slender Perspex windshield that curved around the cockpit, and with great finesse stepped onto the driveway, without even opening the car's small door.

'I'm supposed to be on my way to somewhere called Bishop's Frome. I must have taken a wrong turning. Then I saw this roadside sign back there saying there was a fete on down here, with tea and cakes.' She did a little mock-curtsey. 'So, *voila*, here I am!'

She went up to him and kissed him on the cheek. There was the unmistakable aroma of her expensive French perfume which he remembered of old.

Anthony glanced down at an impressive circular gold badge set in the centre of the car's bonnet. 'What is it?'

'It's a Porsche 550 Spyder. Precursor of the modern Boxster.'

The car's lines were sensuously rounded, terminating in distinctive rear wheel arches, each capped with a conical red brake light. A huge central exhaust pipe projected from the rear, like the flattened bell of a trumpet.

'How old is it?'

'This one was built in 1955. So that would make it 60 years old. Twelve years older than little old me! They only made 90 of them and they're all numbered. Apparently this one competed in the Targa Florio mountain road race around Sicily. There's an enamel badge on the dash.'

He leaned in to study the sparse monocoque interior, which was not unlike the inside of one of the racing sculls he had rowed at Oxford. The aluminium-framed dashboard had only three dials and the tiny squab seats, upholstered in red leather, looked more like modern-day children's car seats. At least half of the car's entire length appeared to be devoted to leg room for the driver and passenger, while the other half – behind the two seat backs – was occupied by a huge vented engine hatch, secured by a pair of leather straps. Clearly an ex-racer, the car still bore large blank white roundels on its doors.

'Where do you put the groceries?'

'Hasn't on-line shopping reached Shropshire, then?' The woman began rolling a red tonneau cover across the cockpit, expertly twisting the chrome toggle clips which secured it to the bodywork. 'I could murder a pot of Earl Grey; care to join me?'

'Eva, you can't leave this car parked here – not right across the car park entrance!'

'Well I'm certainly not taking it into that field. It's only got a ground clearance of nine centimetres, you know? I took the silencer off on a fucking speed bump in Chelsea last month!'

'Well at least just move it onto the verge, would you?'

Grudgingly she did as she was instructed, then finished fitting the cover.

'No hood?'

'Nope.'

'So what happens when it rains?'

'You get wet, you wally!' She took his arm. 'Come on, sweetie, let's go and find the tea tent.'

Eva was several inches shorter than Anthony, with the top of her trim figure attired in a waisted black leather Alexander McQueen bikers' jacket, with quilted shoulders and wide lapels lined with black Persian lamb. Underneath was a revealing open-necked red silk blouse. Her shoes were red suede-strapped wooden wedge sandals. As he looked down at her face, he saw the small band of freckles which ran across the bridge of her nose and the tiny mole above her left cheek. He had forgotten just how alluring those facial blemishes were.

At the end of the drive the couple branched right, passing through a shaded pergola of climbing scented roses, entwined by flowering jasmine. They eventually arrived at an entrance table, set beside the gates to Codrington Manor's grounds. "ALL PROCEEDS WILL GO TO ST GUTHRAC CHURCH TOWER'S RESTORATION AND A NEW SET OF BELLS" proclaimed a large board set in front of the table.

Seated at the table were two elderly ladies, one shaded by a floral parasol. Behind them stood a handsome, dark-haired youth in a smart army cadet corps uniform. Anthony offered one of the ladies a £5 note for Eva's admission and handed her the ticket.

'I'll catch up with you in a couple of minutes if I may; I just want to have a word with this young man. They're doing the teas in the Orangery, by the way. It's just beyond the arboretum.' Eva wandered off.

'Tim — would you do me a great favour?'

'Sure,' said the cadet.

'Go and cover for me at the car park entrance for about 20 minutes, there's a pal? I just want to take that lady for a cup of tea. We're old friends.'

'Right you are, Mr Metcalf.'

He walked off to catch up with Eva, calling back to the boy: 'Just make 'em park tidy in four parallel rows, will you. Right up to the fence with the barley field.' The boy gave a salute of acknowledge- ment and marched smartly off in the direction of the car park, pleased to have been given a job with a bit of responsibility.

As Anthony and Eva strolled through the arboretum, the gleaming white outline of Codrington Manor's majestic Orangery loomed into sight through the trees.

Resting her head lightly on his shoulder, Eva whispered: 'So I've got you all to myself for 20 minutes, have I?'

The lofty, two-storey Orangery was an impressive structure, though clearly of a much later date than the old manor house. Its inspiration could well have been one of the lesser greenhouses in London's Kew Gardens. It positively gleamed in the bright sunshine, with its solid white timber framework and slender glazing bars supporting row upon row of angled glass panels. Urn-shaped lead corner finials, surmounting the posts of the double entrance doors, completed the formal composition.

Inside, the huge space was buzzing with the noise of the fete's visitors. The perimeter was lined with exotic indoor plants: ferns, cacti, orchids, two magnificent specimens of the indoor *ficus benjamanii* and several fruit-bearing orange and lemon trees. Octagonal-patterned cast iron gratings were set into the terracotta pathways.

High above, two sets of electrically-controlled rooflights had been opened, creating a pleasant upward draught. Down at lower levels, bamboo-slatted drapes reduced the glare and solar gain.

Eva headed for a quiet two-seater corner table beneath an orange tree, while Anthony joined the line waiting for cream teas.

The acoustics inside the Orangery had never been intended to accommodate the boisterous throng of well over one hundred fete-goers, all eagerly consuming their cream teas and chatting.

Alongside the glazed entrance doors was a niche containing a marble bust of Sir Josiah Codrington Bt. Beneath it, a plaque recorded the construction dates of the impressive glasshouse: 1835-39. What neither this plaque nor the £5 souvenir guide revealed, was that the Orangery's entire costs and planting had been met from the huge compensation which Sir Josiah (philanderer and habitual gambler) received from the British government in 1833, for the freeing of the 218 slaves who worked on his 300-acre sugar plantation on the Caribbean island of Tobago.

After about ten minutes, Anthony rejoined Eva, carrying a tray. He sat beside her while she poured their teas. Glancing down at her exposed thighs he whispered: 'Eva, can you pull your skirt down a bit; I can almost see your navel.'

Without pausing from her tea-pouring or making any attempt to adjust her skirt line, Eva mumbled: 'My, haven't you got stuffy? I can remember when you used to tell me to lift my skirt higher. Like that time we were in the Savoy Grill and there were four Lebanese businessmen sat at the next table. Married life has certainly dampened your libido!' They drank their teas in silence.

Eventually Anthony's curiosity got the better of him. 'So what brings you to rural Shropshire? Aren't you living in Sweden?'

'Was. Past tense, dear.'

'What's happened to your husband, Mr Carlssen?'

'I've left him in Oslo. Six feet under.'

'I'm so sorry, Eva. What did he do for a living?'

'Do you know, I was never quite sure. Something to do with making working parts for all those wind farms they're littering the North Sea with. Stainless steel sprockets or polycarbonate widgets, or something like that. It certainly made him very rich.'

'Was he your second or third – I've rather lost count.'

'Third.'

Anthony lowered his voice. 'Well, if you don't mind my saying so, Eva, his loss doesn't seem to have affected you greatly.'

Beneath the table, she unhooked one of her sandals and ran a bare foot slowly up his calf. 'You were my great loss.' He spluttered on the remains of a cream scone and attempted to change the subject, although the softly pulsating foot continued to massage his leg.

'So where are you living at the moment?'

'In London, in a hotel.'

'Which one?'

'The Dorchester. But I'm house-hunting.'

'In Shropshire?'

'No, stupid. I just got fed up with dealing with oily London estate agents, so I thought I'd take myself off to the country for a while. I've rented this sweet little cottage at Bishop's Frome for a fortnight. You must come over and see it.' As she re-filled their cups, she added casually: 'By the way, I'm a fully-fledged witch now, you know?'

Anthony picked some crumbs from his plate and attempted the

same degree of nonchalance. 'You don't say. So are they doing OU courses in witchcraft nowadays?'

'There's no need to be sarky, Anthony. If you must know, I had to go up to the Outer Hebrides. There's an active coven up there. Three weeks in a fucking hovel, darling! They live in the most unbelievable squalor. Imagine having to eat toad's entrails and lizard's legs for breakfast! Honestly, I don't know how I survived.'

'A proper coven?'

She finished her tea. 'Yup. My indoctrination ended with a bukakke session at midnight on the last night. Ever done bukakke?'

'Err, no. But I know what's involved. Not my scene at all, I'm afraid.'

'There were 13 guys in my ring, with me in the middle. It was wicked! More tea?'

'No thanks. Can we change the subject, please? You know you really have got a mind like a sewer!'

'You once told me you found my dirty talk delicious.'

Eva leaned across and was about to stroke the back of his hand, when a tall dark-haired woman in an apron approached their table. Ignoring Eva, she addressed Anthony: 'Who's looking after the car park?' she snapped.

'Jack Nugent's son, Tim.'

'Anthony, that boy's far too young to be down there on his own! You'd better go back and relieve him.' She glanced down at Eva, as if only having just noticed that he was sitting with someone.

'Barbara – this is an old friend of mine, Eva Carlssen.' Then for Eva's benefit, he added: 'My wife, Barbara.'

'Pleased to meet you,' said Eva pleasantly, looking up and smiling. Barbara gave a wan smile and nodded. 'By the way, I trust you said "hello" to Lady Codrington at the entrance.'

'I don't think I'd recognise Lady Codrington. What does she look like?'

'She was sat at the ticket table with Deirdre Prosser.'

'You mean the old biddy with the parasol and the *pince-nez*, who looks like Miss Havisham?'

'That's no way to speak of our hostess! Now when you and your... friend here have finished your teas, I'd like you to resume your duties in the car park. And send Tim up here, would you? We're running out of clean cups and saucers; he can help with the washing up. I'd better be getting back to the kitchens.' She nodded at Eva and walked off, wiping her hands on her pinafore.

Eva swung her fishnet-clad legs around from beneath the table and brushed some crumbs from her mini-tartan. 'A pinafore suits her,' she observed tartly. 'Doesn't she play the part of a skivvy in that dreadful Edwardian costume soap on TV on Sunday nights?'

'"*Hotel Imperial*". Yes, she's been in both series.'

'Seems to spend most of her time either polishing wine glasses or else she's on her knees cleaning out fire grates!'

'That's what skivvies did in those days.'

Eva stood up. Two elderly gentlemen at an adjoining table – one wearing a dog collar – took a last admiring glance at her slender legs.

'Right, well I'm going to take a stroll around the grounds. You'd better be off back to your car parking duties, or you'll be getting a reprimand from wifey. And that would never do. Chop, chop!'

Five minutes later, Anthony found Tim Nugent nervously standing guard over Eva's Porsche, surrounded by a gaggle of admiring young petrolheads. The youth seemed relieved to see him return and the boys stood back respectfully, assuming the sports car to be his.

'Thanks for holding the fort, Tim. Any problems?'

'No, it's been real quiet. I don't suppose we've had more than 15 cars come in since you left.'

'Mrs Metcalf has asked if you'd mind going up to the kitchens behind the Orangery. I gather they're running out of clean cups and saucers and she could do with some help with the washing up.'

'Right you are.' Tim marched smartly off in the direction of the Orangery.

When Eva eventually reappeared, she began un-buttoning the tonneau covering the cockpit of the little sports car.

'So where do you put your luggage, when you go on holiday?' Anthony enquired, wandering across from the car park entrance. The petrolheads were now admiring Eva.

'There's hardly any room under the front bonnet – that's mostly taken up by leg room. I tend to travel light and as I'm always on my own, I just plonk two or three cases on the passenger seat. Or else I send them on ahead.'

'And aren't there any tools?'

'Darling, this was a sports-racing car! German mechanics took care of all that sort of thing.'

'So what happens when you break down?'

'I stand at the side of the road and look helpless. It nearly always works! Though sometimes – usually with white van drivers – it can lead to complications.' Eva winked as she tucked the rolled-up tonneau behind the driver's seat. Anthony didn't need to ask what "complications" might involve.

Clasping the edge of the curved plastic windshield, she executed a neat high-kick, planting her left leg squarely on the squab of the driving seat, followed by her other leg. This elegant manoeuvre momentarily exposed not only her trim posterior, but the fact that she was wearing no knickers beneath her mini-tartan. It was an omission which didn't go unnoticed amongst the sniggering schoolboys standing close by.

Eva remained standing inside the car as she slipped on her elbow-length driving gloves, waiting for Anthony to draw close, to bid her farewell. Puckering up her lips, she closed her eyes.

'Kissy kissy?' But he only brushed her cheek lightly with his lips, before stepping back.

'Lovely to see you again, Eva. Drive carefully.'

Eva deftly slid down onto the bucket seat and turned on the ignition, firing the Porsche into life. Above its excited, rasping crackle he could just make out her words: 'I'll love you and leave you, my darling. Bye!' Then slipping the dome-topped gear shift into first gear, she let in the clutch and sped off up the lane in another cloud of dust.

After seeing off the last of the fete's visitors from the car park, Anthony drove his Volvo estate car round to the back of the Orangery, where he collected several boxfuls of crockery, together with general litter, which Tim helped him to load.

He told Barbara he would go on ahead and organise supper for them at home. 'And don't forget to feed the dog,' she called out as he drove off.

Kynaston Barn lay about three miles outside the market town of Ludlow. It was an 18th century stone-built field barn, which the previous owners had converted into a spacious two-storey house. Recycled materials and traditional decorations abounded throughout the open-planned interior.

The house phone rang just after 9.00p.m., as the couple were finishing a cold salmon supper in the kitchen. Barbara took the call.

'Mrs Metcalf? Walter Redknapp. I'm sorry to ring you at this late hour, as I imagine you must be exhausted.'

'That's perfectly all right, Walter.'

'Well Doris and I have just finished counting this afternoon's takings. And from the gate receipts, tea and cake sales and the raffle, there's a grand total of £2,867.47p. As the Patron of the church bells appeal, we wanted to let you know straight away!'

'That's wonderful!'

'It is, isn't it? What's more, do you know that in one of the collecting buckets from the entrance gate, there was a cheque for £250!'

'I say, how generous. And who was the donor?'

'It's rather hard to make out the signature, as it's very scrawled. But it looks like "Carlssen".'

Barbara hesitated. She felt like telling the appeal's treasurer to tear the cheque up, but thought better of it. 'Well thank you for the call, Walter. And for all your hard work today. And do thank Doris too for helping out in the kitchens this afternoon, won't you?'

'I will. Good night, Mrs Metcalf.'

As she was making herself a bedtime drink, Barbara called out to her husband in the big sitting room, where he was perusing the Sunday newspapers, with their fluffy-haired Sheltie curled up at his feet. 'Well you'll be pleased to hear that the tarty woman you were talking to in the Orangery has been throwing her largesse around!'

She swept past him with her mug, heading for the staircase. 'I'm off to bed.'

He glanced up. At this late hour, petty verbal sparring matches about "that tarty woman" were rather pointless and he returned to his weekly Sudoku. 'Right you are. See you in the morning.'

From the stairs, Barbara called: 'You haven't forgotten that I'm off early filming on Tuesday, have you Anthony?'

He lowered the magazine and looked over the top of his spectacles. 'Sorry, it had completely slipped my mind. Tuesday, you say?'

With irritation, she paused at the half-landing. 'Three days. I told you. They've decided to re-shoot one of my scenes because the lighting's wrong. I won't be back until Thursday at the earliest. I'll probably have to set off before 6.00a.m.'

'You'd better take the Volvo, then. I can use the little Fiat this week to get into Ludlow.'

'Thanks. I'll keep you posted on my movements once I get to the studios at Watford. Good night.'

# II

## *Florian's*

IT WAS JUST after 9.00a.m. when Anthony parked the blue Fiat 500 in his usual spot behind Ludlow's Market Square. Traders were already setting up their stalls beneath the blue-and-white striped awnings. He waved to his friend Terry Daniels, who ran a bric-a-brac stall and headed for his book shop on the east side of square.

The blue-painted, double-fronted façade of "Train Spotters" was one of Ludlow Market's most distinctive shops: a secondhand book emporium catering for rail enthusiasts. In the style of an old locomotive name badge, the sign on the shop's glazed entrance door, in gilded lettering, read: "Glorious Railway Nostalgia." Projecting from the brickwork above the shop's fascia was a replica of a red-and-white semaphore-style railway signal.

The shop's left-hand window display was a cornucopia of railway ephemera, from vintage travel posters to postcards, badges, train drivers' hats and lamps, and several old jigsaw puzzles featuring the Flying Scotsman under full steam.

The right-hand window display had been Anthony's brain-child. As a backdrop to a window filled with railway-themed books, he had organised a 3m-high blow-up of the colour cover of the history of the construction of the trans-Siberian Railway, *To the Edge of the World*. The enlarged photograph showed a fearsome looking ancient black-painted Russian locomotive, steaming through the snow of the Russian Steppes. It was an arresting image that could be seen across the square.

Anthony Metcalf unlocked the shop door, switched on the interior lights, scooped up the mail from the door mat and flipped over the hanging plywood cut-out of a loco announcing: "OPEN".

Front-to-back, the book store was about 20 metres deep, terminating with a narrow passageway to a back office and a tiny kitchenette. The shop's right-hand wall was reserved for bookshelves and displays, with a long central island labelled "vintage collectibles".

Alongside the rear passageway was an old mahogany plan chest, containing more than one hundred original blue linen engineering drawings from the office of I. K. Brunel. They had all been made at the time of the construction of the Great West Railway. Anthony had bought them some years previously as a 'job lot', when Network Rail was clearing out some old offices in Swindon. Collectors willingly paid £15 or £20 for Indian ink drawings of GWR signal boxes and bridges.

Down the left-hand wall of the shop was a huge black-and-white photo of the record-breaking speed run by the A4-class locomotive *Mallard*, seen in full flight outside Grantham. The grainy 75-year-old image captured the moment when the train was completing a high-speed water intake – travelling at over 100mph – via track-level nozzles set under the front of the engine, that scooped up water from metal troughs laid between the lines. Taking on water on the move during record attempts improved times. When the engine's tank was full, surplus water was dramatically sprayed out sideways, like waves made by a speedboat's bow. Beneath the *Mallard* blow-up were labelled racks of train CDs and DVDs, flanked by a pair of old LNER platform benches.

Anthony riffled through the incoming mail, sorting bills from orders. The latter were invariably dealt with the same day, while the former would usually take at least a fortnight to be settled. Before slipping into the back kitchenette to make his first tea of the morning, he dropped a tape cassette into the player beneath the counter. While despising what he called the 'lift car music' played in supermarkets, he liked to add authentic train sounds to the shop's atmosphere.

Just as the kettle was boiling, he heard the "ting" of the front entrance door opening. Checking his watch (true train spotters, in his experience, were seldom up and about before 11.00a.m.), he moved to the entrance passage to see who his visitor was.

Framed in the sun-lit doorway stood Eva. Her striking outfit was a pair of hip-hugging black leather trousers with a plaited belt of silver thread, below a cleavage-revealing open cream silk blouse, topped by a trim powder blue double-breasted suede blazer. Her red hair was held up by a silver and tortoise shell grip and her emerald ear studs exactly matched the colour of her eyes. It was an outfit more suited to Bond Street than Ludlow Market.

Anthony set his mug down on a shelf and sauntered down to greet the early-morning visitor. As he drew closer, he saw that around her neck, on a silver chain, was a silver owl pendant.

'Hello stranger – what brings you into Ludlow at this hour?'

'Good morning, sweetie! I need a new handbag – but of course I didn't realise that nowhere in this sleepy little place opens before 10.00a.m. Do you feel like treating me to a coffee? I could murder a double espresso.' She shimmied towards him and as they met, she ran one hand slowly down his hip. 'Is that a railway timetable in your pocket, or are you just pleased to see me?'

'You seem in remarkably good spirits, I must say.'

'*Bien sûr!* I feel in the mood to celebrate. Come on, let's go and grab that coffee and I'll tell you all about it.'

'I'm sorry, Eva, but it's out of the question: I've only just this minute opened the shop.'

'Anthony – don't be so stuffy. Chill out a bit. Anyway, who's going to want to buy...' she turned to scan the stock to hand, picking up a dog-eared catalogue of engine numbers '...a used 1954 Ian Allan loco list, at 9.30 in the bloody morning?'

'Lots of people; you'd be surprised.'

She snatched his hand. 'Well then, they can form a queue outside till we get back, can't they? Come on!'

Anthony fished his key chain from his pocket and went to lock the shop door.

'No coat?' She gestured at a crumpled blue jacket draped over the stool behind the counter. He dutifully collected it and she helped him slip it on. 'I do so love this jacket. Remember when I bought it for you in Covent Garden?'

'Vaguely.'

'Little wifey not know how to use an iron?' she asked, running a hand down one of its crumpled sleeves.

'Eva, I do wish you'd stop referring to Barbara as "little wifey"; she's got a name you know? Now come on, I mustn't be long.'

Anthony and Eva headed down Market Street in the direction of Florian's, Ludlow's famed and antiquated restaurant and cake shop. It was quiet when they entered, with only a couple of stalwart *Daily Telegraph* readers in evidence.

As they took a table by the open fire, Eva looked around and observed tartly: 'This place is like a time warp! I'd say it's due for a make-over.'

'No thank you very much! We certainly don't want Kevin McLoud down here ripping out 75 years of character.'

'Who's Kevin McLoud?'

'Have you been living on Mars for the last five years?'

'Oslo. Same thing.'

'He's a TV design guru.'

'Like Conran?'

'Hardly. Terence Conran was avuncular and knowledgeable when it came to modern design. McLoud's just an infuriating poseur.'

Two pretty young waitresses hovered in the background gossiping, before one stepped forward to take their order. She smiled at Anthony Metcalf, who glanced quizzically at Eva, who was studying the menu.

'Eggs Benedict, but on a buttered bagel and not toast, please; and a cafetière.' The girl scribbled on her order pad. 'And for you, Mr Metcalf?'

'Just a cappuccino, Julia, but with my usual double shot?'

'Certainly, sir.'

After the waitress had left with their order, Eva whispered slyly: 'Julia, eh? You two seem very friendly.'

'I come in here most days and she usually serves me. That's all.'

'Sure that's all? Bit of teenage skirt in the town? Nice legs, cute bum? Sure she doesn't come by the bookshop after she's finished work for a quickie in your back office?'

'I've told you this before – you really should check that jealousy of yours.'

'Jealous? *Moi*?' She hissed a mini-screech, causing the irritated rustle of a nearby *Daily Telegraph*.

'Yes, Eva, you. You're as jealous as Hera. And as vengeful. Always have been.'

'Name an example.'

'Amsterdam.'

She gave a pained half-smile and fixed him with a steely squint. 'Remind me?'

'That lovely little Rijsttafel restaurant - in the red light district? We were having a delicious meal – until you decided I was ogling the waitress.'

'Oh that. Well I had every right to be upset! Making eyes at that slutty little tart. She was practically falling out of that blouse!'

'That was a traditional Dutch Indonesian costume. That's where Rijsttafel originates.'

'All my eye and Betty Martin. That was no more a Dutch Indonesian costume than Liberace's glitter cat suit! You've just got a kink about waitresses.'

'As if I'd be likely to flirt with a waitress – either in Amsterdam or here Ludlow. Get real!'

'Anthony, you've got so stuffy since we lived together.'

'And you're a fantasist; we NEVER lived together!'

'What about Corsica?'

'That was just a bloody holiday!'

She exhaled with exasperation, then picked up her fork and studied it, pouting.

'So what exactly are you celebrating?'

'Three things actually. I had a call this morning from the Secretary of the Midland Automobile Club, to say that my application to participate in a Women's All-Comers hill climb competition at Shelsley Walsh next Sunday has been accepted.'

'In the Spyder?'

'Yup. Fancy coming as my mechanic?'

'Sorry, no can do. Next Sunday I'm doing our annual stock take.'

Eva pouted again. '*Quelle dommage!*' Anthony remembered how cunningly persuasive her entreaties could be when preceded by a pout.

'And the second thing?'

She gently fingered the silver owl which hung at her neck. He noticed that its eyes were oval cabochon-cut emeralds which matched the centre of her ear studs.

'Well, in the post there was a letter from my solicitor, to say that my offer on the house in London I want to buy has been accepted. Isn't that wonderful? I've been getting fed up living in a hotel – especially one where ninety per cent of the other guests are lecherous Arabs who can't keep their hands to themselves!'

'So whereabouts is it, this house you're buying?'

'Hyde Park – well, just off: Connaught Square.'

'I say, how very chic! A whole house?'

'Yup, three storeys plus a basement and an attic. And a huge garden. Needs some work done on it though. The downside is that it's three doors down from the bloody Blairs.'

'THE Blairs?'

''fraid so. They're hardly my favourite couple.'

'Mine neither.' He paused and then smiled. 'Still, there is one plus side to having them as your neighbours.'

'What's that?'

'As they're just about the most reviled couple on the planet, I think you can assume that security in your square is going to be of a pretty high order.'

She considered his theory for a moment. 'I suppose you're right. I hadn't looked at it like that. You old clever clogs!'

'And number three?'

'Sorry?'

'The third reason you're celebrating.'

She gave a little shrug and fluttered her long eyelashes. 'Well they say good things come in threes, don't they? So meeting you again after six years has got to be the third reason.'

She reached out to place her hand on his, just as the waitress arrived with their order. As if to punish the girl for the unwarranted intrusion, Eva picked up her fork and handed it to her with a wan smile. 'I wonder if you'd mind fetching me another – this one's soiled.'

'Certainly, madam'.

Eva tucked into her breakfast with gusto, while Anthony patiently watched, surreptitiously checking the time.

'Meet anyone after Mr Carlssen passed away?'

She mopped up the last of the egg yolk. 'I'm afraid not. I've tried dating agencies and lonely hearts columns. Even joined an online swingers club, would you believe? They're all either moronic losers or guys who get a kick out of cheating on their wives!'

'Really?'

'I met one fellow; went out with him three times, actually. Quite cultivated. Took me to the ballet at Covent Garden. And he was a good performer in the sack, I have to admit. Then I discovered he was a fucking vicar!'

'Somehow, I can't see you as a vicar's wife, Eva.'

'Nor me, darling. Got time to order me another cafetière?'

'I'm afraid not. I really must be getting back. It's gone 10.00a.m.'

'Honestly, Anthony – marriage has made you so boring!'

'Leave off! I've got to earn a living, you know.' With obvious irritation, he signalled to the waitress to bring the bill.

'So how's it doing – this bookshop of yours - profit-wise?'

'So-so. Ludlow folk are foodies really. But summer tourism makes up for it. I'm just about keeping my head above water.'

'With or without wifey's help?'

'Without, thank you very much!'

'How did you and Barbara meet?'

'She was in a production of Shaw's *Joan of Arc* in London. It was just after I'd quit teaching. I just loved her performance. Saw it three times, then I hung around the stage door for her autograph. We just clicked. We've been married six years now.'

Eva sniffed. 'I'd hardly say her figure resembles the diminutive Maid of Orleans. So she caught you on the rebound, so to speak.'

'Rebound? From whom?'

Eva spluttered: 'From ME, you nana!'

It was tactless to remind her that their torrid affair had barely survived four months, the last weeks of which were purgatory.

The waitress delivered their bill. 'Were the eggs to your satisfaction, madam?'

Eva dabbed the corners of her mouth with her serviette, without disturbing her cerise gloss lipstick. 'Very good indeed, thank you.' The half-smile was insincere.

Anthony went to place a £10 note on the saucer, but Eva pushed it aside. 'My treat – I insist.' He added a coin as a tip and stood up.

She took his arm as they left through the front cake shop. Outside on the pavement, Anthony mumbled: 'Oh Christ, that's torn it!'

'What's up?'

'Mrs Redknapp was buying some cakes in there.'

'Who's Mrs Redknapp?'

'She only happens to be the biggest gossip in Ludlow.'

'Forget it: small town, small-minded people! Wait until I've moved into Connaught Square. You can come to stay with me there and nobody will bat an eyelid – not even those pious Blairs. Anyway, I've got news for you, sweetie. She may be an old gossip, but your Mrs Redknapp is in the light'.

'What's "in the light"?'

'Enlightened. One of us.' She squeezed his arm extra tight and whispered: 'She's a witch.'

'Don't be bloody preposterous, Eva. I know Doris Redknapp is a silly, gossiping old trout, but I think that's one fantasy too far. Wife of one of the pillars of local society, who is captain of the golf club, a Rotarian, a mason and honorary treasurer of Barbara's church bells appeal to boot.'

'What's that got to do with the price of beef dripping? Harold Shipman was a doctor!'

'Anyway, how do you know? Was she in your coven in the Hebrides?'

'I saw her aura in the cake shop.'

'Her what?' Anthony unlocked the bookshop's door.

'It's like an iridescent purple halo.'

Once back inside "Train Spotters" Anthony soon realised that he hadn't shaken off his ex-lover. She was now pacing around his shop, examining the merchandise. She paused to listen to the tape cassette that was playing.

'What's THAT?'

'What's what?'

'That awful noise.'

'It's not awful noise. It's music!'

'Call that music? I thought for a minute your neighbours had got the builders in.'

'Very droll. That happens to be the second movement of a minimalist concerto by the American composer Steve Reich...'

'Never heard of him.'

'...who is regarded as America's greatest living composer. And this is probably his best known work.'

'What's it called?'

'*Different Trains*'. At that moment, the soundtrack lapsed into the haunting wail of an American loco's steam whistle.

'Funny subject – trains – for a retired English master to choose for the theme of a bookshop, wasn't it?' She was idly flicking through the DVDs.

Anthony busied himself at the till, totting up the previous week's takings. 'After I was forced to take early retirement from Birch Cross, this place came on the market, as the owners wanted to retire. I decided I'd try a themed bookshop. Hence the trains.'

'Do you miss teaching?'

'Of course I do. It was my vocation; ever since coming down from Oxford. I miss it terribly.'

'Ever apply for another position?'

'There wasn't any point. Things like that spread through the school governors' grapevine like a bushfire. I knew I was finished. And as the severance terms they offered me – plus the inevitable gagging clause – were pretty generous, I decided to go quietly. The money helped me to set up this place. Any way, it wasn't against the law what I did with that boy, you know? He was over age and he'd consented. It's just that the headmaster and the chairman of the board of governors were both homophobic bigots.'

'Have you ever told Barbara?'

'Of course not!'

Eva took a DVD to the counter and handed Anthony a £10 note. 'Be terrible if she ever found out, wouldn't it?'

'That's hardly likely, after all these years.'

'I wouldn't be so sure, sweetie!'

He ignored the ominous threat, then chuckled when he saw her choice of film. 'Eva, you really are incorrigible! Your old sexual antenna never lets you down, does it?'

'What on earth are you talking about?'

He held up the box for her to read the title: *Closely Observed Trains*. 'You've only selected the sexiest film in the entire shop! Ever seen it?'

She giggled as she slipped it into her shoulder bag. 'No. But I can't imagine how an old black-and-white Czech movie about trains could possibly be sexy!'

Ringing up the till and handing her the receipt, he smiled. 'Believe you me, it is!'

'Ooo good, I'll watch it in bed tonight. Care to join me?'

'Sorry, but no. Now what about that handbag you came into town to buy?'

'I can see I'm not wanted.' She sniffed haughtily as the phone rang. 'Ay up, and that'll be little wifey.'

Anthony was mildly surprised to discover that the caller was indeed Barbara. He dismissed it as a lucky guess.

'Where on earth have you been – I rang the shop at 9.20a.m. but there was no answer.'

'Err, I had to take some orders to the Post Office.'

'What, first thing on a Monday morning?'

He shifted nervously as he saw Eva smiling at his lie.

'I'm going over to Mother's. Poor dear, she's got problems with her carer. I just wanted to remind you again that the new gardener starts tomorrow morning. You hadn't forgotten, had you?'

He had. 'Err, no, of course not, Barbara. When do you expect to be back today?'

'I've no idea. I suggest you get your own supper. I'll probably eat with Mummy.'

'OK. I'll see you later. Bye.'

Eva heard the final exchange from the doorway on her way out. 'Home alone, eh? You make sure you behave yourself. Right, now which is the best shop for handbags in this burgh?'

'"Just My Bag". Top of Broad Street, just down from the Butter Cross.'

'OK, sweetie. I'd better love you and leave you.' She blew him a kiss. 'I may ring you later. *Ciao.*'

Trade was sluggish throughout the morning and Anthony was reluctant to even shut the shop for half-an-hour to dash out to buy a sandwich. Instead, he snacked on crisps and chocolate biscuits. Neither Barbara nor Eva called.

Terry the cheery Cockney market trader appeared shortly before Anthony was preparing to close up, swinging a bulky plastic carrier bag.

'How's trade?'

'Dead as a Dodo.'

'Really? I thought I spotted a posh dolly leaving here mid-morning.'

'She only spent £10 on one DVD and took up an hour of my time.'

'Nice gams though.'

'An old flame.'

'Really? Lucky you. Right, when you've got a moment, I'd like you to cast your expert eye over this little number.' He hoisted the plastic bag onto the counter. 'An old dear sold me a box full of junk on Saturday for a fiver and I found this in the bottom.'

Anthony peered into the bag at a big leather-bound volume. 'Hello – might this be an old Bradshaw, by any chance?'

'Seems so, by the fly-leaf. But it's pretty far gone. Do you know anything about 'em?'

'Only that they're every train spotter's bible. In good nick, that is...' He pulled it out. '... which this one clearly isn't. If it was in better condition, Michael Portillo would probably wet himself!'

Anthony placed it on the counter. The back cover was missing, but it was certainly a Victorian edition of the famous European railway timetable.

'I'd say this could be something special. Why don't I take it over and show it to Cyril my bookbinder?' He held it up to the light. It appeared that, at one time, even the edges of its pages had been gilded. 'The spine's knackered too. If Cyril could work his magic on it, we might be able to sell it on eBay. What do you think?'

'Why not? Let's give it a go, shall we?'

'Right you are. Leave it with me and I'll call by to see him on my way home later in the week. I'll let you know what he suggests.'

He stuck the Bradshaw at the back of a shelf below the counter and switched the tape player off. Anthony couldn't bring himself to check the day's till roll. He knew it would be less than £100.

The drive along the wooded back roads from Ludlow to the Metcalfs' converted barn at Kynaston was uneventful, but thoughts of Eva's surprising reappearance in his life kept crossing his mind. He wondered just how much of a coincidence her arrival at Sunday's fete at Codrington Manor had really been.

As soon as he got out of the Fiat to open the garage door, Ben the Sheltie began barking furiously from inside the house. He parked the car and let himself in, to an ecstatic reception from the dog.

No sooner had he started to prepare himself a quick salad supper than he heard the "ping" of his mobile phone, registering an incoming message. He poured himself a fortifying glass of wine in preparation for fresh orders from Major Barbara.

Instead, the message was from Eva. "You were so right about the Czech train movie! Loved the naughty scene with the rubber franking stamp. Wish you were here in bed watching it with me! Have sent a little parcel in the post to the shop. Eva xxx"

# III

## *Russian Windfall*

WATCHED BY HIS faithful little dog, Anthony was feeding goldfish when the new gardener pulled up in his Land Rover on the Tuesday morning. The long case clock in the barn was striking 8.00a.m. Barbara had left two hours earlier.

The driver jumped out enthusiastically. He was wearing crisp blue overalls (bearing the logo of a Swedish chainsaw manufacturer), over polished black leather boots with steel toe caps. He was clean-shaven and weather-beaten, and from his erect stance, Anthony guessed that the he had probably once been in the regular army.

'Mr Metcalf? Mike Green. Your wife told me to be here at eight sharp.' He proffered a rock-hard handshake.

'Welcome to Kynaston Barn, Mike. Did you find us OK?'

'No probs.'

'Come far?'

'Clun.'

'Quite a way, then. Well, we're very pleased you could fit us in. How long have you lived up there?'

'Man and boy, Mr Metcalf, man and boy.'

'So you must have known the famed playwright John Osborne?'

'Oh yes. I knew Mr Osborne. I worked for him, briefly.'

'What was he like? I'm told he was a bit prickly towards locals?'

'Mardy? Yes, you could say that. I'm afraid I couldn't get on with the gentleman. I've no objection to customers checking up on my work;

they've every right. But one time I caught 'im measuring the length of the blades of grass what I'd just cut. With a tape measure! 'e said I needed to set my mower up 'igher else I'd wreck 'is lawn. So I left.'

Anthony rather admired a man who could walk out on the curmudgeonly playwright. 'Right, shall we do a quick tour? I need to be away just before 9.00a.m.'

'Right you be.'

Shadowed by Ben, they strolled around the mature half-acre garden which surrounded the old barn. At the conclusion, he warned: 'And whatever you do, don't touch the roses – they're my wife's exclusive domain!'

'Right you be.'

'Even if they're crawling with greenfly, just leave her a note to tell her. I'd suggest you always make cutting the grass and edging the verges your first job - weather permitting. Put the cut grass in the two green composting bins behind the garage. In the autumn, rake the leaves from the drive. The mower and the strimmer are both in the garage, along with any feeds and dressings you'll need.'

Anthony checked his watch as their tour ended back by the fish pond. 'Now there's one little task I'd like us to tackle together, if you're willing?'

'What would that be, Mr Metcalf?'

He nodded at the tall evergreen hedge running along one of the garden's boundaries. 'That Leylandii. I hate the bloody thing! The last owners planted it and it's got out of control. It needs pruning at least four times a year.'

'So what was you thinking: grub it up?'

'Unfortunately, we'd never get away with it. That hedge fronts onto a bridle path that's used by local ramblers. They'd blow the whistle on us to the council's tree conservation department, for certain. And if we put in a formal application, I'm pretty sure we'd get turned down.'

'So what are you suggesting?'

'Poison its roots.'

Mike Green pursed his lips and sucked in his breath with alarm.

'I know, I know. I don't like killing living organisms either, Mike. But believe you me, this thing's become a liability. The trimmings won't compost and carting them off by trailer to the local tip is costing us a small fortune.

'So my plan is to take out a shallow trench here on the garden side – say 20 x 20cms – then water its roots with the strongest weed killer I can buy. Maybe give it two doses over a fortnight. Come the autumn we should be able to spot the die-back. And with any luck, it'll be a gonner come the spring. If the neighbours should comment, I'll say a heavy frost must have got it.'

'Right you be, Mr Metcalf. If I 'ave time, would you like me to start on the trench today?'

'If you could, that would be great. Set the turfs and the topsoil aside, will you? Once we've given it its two doses, we'll need to backfill and replace the turfs. Hide the evidence, so to speak.'

The gardener gave a wry smile. 'I'm with you.'

'When I've bought the weed killer, I'll leave it for you in the garage. Next to the big box of bone meal on the top shelf, at the back.'

'Don't you keep your garage locked?'

'No, I know we should, but when we're out we just pull the up-and-over door down. By the way, there's a wash room and toilet at the back which you're welcome to use.'

Planting his hands deep in his pockets, the gardener looked up at the tiled roof of the old stone-clad barn. 'Nice place you've got here, Mr Metcalf. Tucked away, too.'

'Yes, we like it here. It's very peaceful.'

'Been here long?'

'Nearly six years. Since Mrs Metcalf and I got married. I moved up here to open a book shop in Ludlow. "Train Spotters" – I expect you know it.'

'In the Market Square? Yes I know the one.'

'Well, I'd better be getting off to open it up.' He led the reluctant Sheltie back into the house, collected his mobile phone from the kitchen table and left to drive into Ludlow.

The post which awaited Anthony at the shop comprised three bills and an bulky brown envelope bearing the town council's logo. There was also a big jiffy bag, with Eva's distinctive handwriting on its label. It was soft and flexible to the touch.

From inside the jiffy bag, he withdrew the pair of black fishnet stockings which Eva had been wearing at the fete. Attached to one of its grip-tops was a small pink card which read:

*Thought you might like to have these with you in bed tonight for company, as you're home alone. E x.*

He paused, pondering how Eva had discerned Barbara's absence. Then copying the return address on a scrap of paper, he popped the stockings back in the bag and pushed it under the shop counter.

The council's letter was an altogether different kettle of fish. It read like the opening salvo in what promised to be a protracted – and expensive – bureaucratic negotiation, to enforce the shop's proprietor "to modify the entrance doorway in order to provide disabled access".

The letter itself (running to five closely-typed pages) quoted Acts of Parliament and ministry directives, listed periods of consultation and representation, and concluded with a thinly-veiled threat of "enforcement procedures" which might ultimately be invoked in the event of "non-compliance". Slipping it back into its envelope, Anthony scribbled across the cover: "Visit solicitor."

Shortly after his first tea break, he took a call from Barbara in the shop's kitchenette. She seemed in good spirits, though she said that due to alterations to the set (which he could hear going on in the background) her three-day filming session was likely to finish late on Thursday evening.

'Now tell me: how did it go with the new gardener?'

'Fine. He seems like a very capable fellow.'

'Did you tell him not to touch my roses?'

'Of course, Barbara.'

'... and that he's always to check the peony frames after thunderstorms?'

'I did.' He hoped he wasn't going to be taken through the entire "remember to tell the new gardener" check list.

'Seen anything of that tarty woman?'

'Do you mean Eva?'

'"Mutton-dressed-as-lamb", as Deirdre Prosser described her on Sunday.'

'No, why should I?'

'Just wondered, that's all. Right, I'd better get back. I'll ring you later in the week, probably when you're home, as it'll be a bit quieter.'

As he sauntered back into the shop, he encountered a gaggle of uniformed schoolboys from the local academy, avidly examining his stock of DVDs. Schoolboy train spotters were part of his most loyal clientele.

One of the youngsters left the huddle and brought an Ian Allan guide to the counter. It was priced at £1 inside the flyleaf. 'Alright if I have it for 50p, as it's a bit knocked about?' the boy enquired cheekily.

'Go on then.' Anthony dropped the coin in the till drawer and gave the boy his receipt. The party hurried out of the shop, laughing. Later in the morning, when tidying the record and film racks, Anthony discovered a gaping hole in his stock, where at least six DVDs had been.

Before closing the shop to go for lunch at Florian's, he put in a quick call to Cyril Mumford, the jovial old bookbinder who he hoped would be able to restore Terry's Victorian Bradshaw. Anthony arranged to call to see him the next day.

A dishevelled individual, who could easily have been a doss house vagrant, was standing in the shop's doorway when he returned from lunch.

The middle-aged man had a dirty black rucksack slung over his shoulder and smelt strongly of beer. His grimy green windcheater was festooned with plastic lapel badges: from "Stop the War" to "Save the Children of Gaza". He wore a khaki forage cap and beside a traditional red Cuban star was another plastic badge, reading: "JC4PM".

Anthony was expecting to be touched for a pound for a cup of tea. But the reason for the man's visit to "Train Spotters" was altogether different.

'Got some stuff in here I thought you might be interested in, governor,' the man slurred, following Anthony into the shop.

With some difficulty, the tramp extracted from his rucksack a small battered cardboard box, placing it in the centre of the counter top, as if preparing to perform a conjuring trick. Slowly, he lifted the four flaps, one at a time. He nodded at the contents. 'Take a look at them, will you?'

The box contained around a hundred postcards, all stored in individual clear plastic envelopes. The first one Anthony pulled out showed, in a sepia hue, the main façade of Moscow's Yaroslavsky railway station. By the appearance of the clothes of the passers-by in front of the huge terminus, he judged that the picture had been taken in the early part of the twentieth century. 'Wow! Are they all like this?'

The shabby man seemed pleased. 'Mostly. All Russian, as far as I can make out, from the stamps and postmarks.'

There were stamped and franked cards from Samara and Omsk, Skovorodino and Irkutsk, Vladivostok and St Petersburg. There were also several views of the mighty *SS Baikal* crashing through the ice of Lake Baikal in winter.

'Nice little collection you've got here, my friend.'

Nodding towards the shop front, the vagrant observed: 'I noticed your window display the other day. I figured you might be interested in buying some Russian postcards.'

'I most certainly would. Mind if I take them all out?'

'Carry on.'

Via a halting cross-examination, Anthony learned that the man (who was living rough) had inherited the collection from his grandmother, who, in turn had been left them by her mother. This Shropshire woman had been married to a Scottish railway engineer who worked for Armstrong Whitworth, the Newcastle-upon-Tyne engineers who had supplied the Russians with the 4000-ton ice-breaking steamer *SS Baikal*. The ship was used by the operators of the trans-Siberian railway to transport trains and their carriages across Lake Baikal in winter.

The Scottish engineer, Anthony was told, had been sent to Listvyanka to supervise the re-assembly of the steamer's 7000 steel components which had all been fabricated in Newcastle-upon-Tyne, assembled, dismantled, numbered and put into wooden packing cases. It had taken three years to re-build the *SS Baikal* in a Russian shipyard, before it was finally put into service on the great lake.

Anthony began returning the cards to the box. 'So it was your great-grandfather, sending all these postcards back home to his wife in Shropshire, who unwittingly created this amazing collection?'

'Seems so.' The tramp seemed flattered by the compliment.

'So what d'you suppose they're worth, governor?'

'Hard to say. At a specialist auction, you could easily get £200 – perhaps more – if the bidding was keen. I'd say the ones of the *Baikal* are particularly rare. You could try putting them on eBay.'

'What's that?'

'It's the internet's version of an auction room. But global.'

'I ain't got a computer. I just thought you might be willing to take 'em off me. How about 50p a card?'

'How many are there?'

'Ninety-six.'

'Would you be happy with £50?'

The tramp could hardly contain himself, grinning to reveal an irregular set of tar-stained teeth. 'Fifty quid would do very nicely, governor!'

The transaction was completed and the man tucked five crisp £10 notes into his shirt pocket. 'Seen a tidy anorak over there in the market that'll do me for the winter.' Anthony suspected that the money would be invested in barley wines first. As the tramp shuffled out, the phone rang. It was Eva.

'Daaaarling! I've been waiting all day for you to ring to thank me for my pressie! Didn't you get them?' She was clearly inebriated.

'Sorry Eva. It's been a bit hectic here today. Yes, I got the stockings. It was a nice thought. Thank you.'

'They're the ones I had on on Sunday. And I haven't washed them.'

'Really? You sound very jolly. Sun over the yard arm early today?'

'Something like that. I've been sunbathing in the garden. We're not overlooked here, so I didn't have a cossie on. Had a couple of little drinkies.'

'So I gather.'

'Why not come over? I could cook you supper.'

'Sorry, no can do. I've got to get back home to feed the dog. Barbara's off filming.'

'Boring! Hey, remember that time I cooked you my speciality: *filet be boeuf au poivre avec cèpes*? And remember what we did after that supper? With you sat at the dining table and me kneeling on the carpet in front of you?'

'Oh Eva - that was a long time ago. A lot of water's flowed under the bridge since then, you know.'

'Suppose so.' He heard the clink of a bottle neck touching a glass. He very nearly added 'And wine too, I dare say.'

'Corsica was wonderful, wasn't it? Remember that deserted cove where we went skinny-dipping?'

'That was a long time ago, too.'

'When's wifey due back?'

'Thursday or Friday.'

'My, my. Does it take that long to film her backside cleaning out a fire grate?'

'I think there's a bit more to it than that, actually.'

'How about we sneak off together for a little holiday? Just you and me?'

'Eva: You never give up, do you?'

'Anthony dearest: if you knew your Zodiac signs, you'd know that we Taurians are a determined lot.'

'It's out of the question. Anyway, I've got nobody to cover for me.'

'Darling: just do what the Spanish do in the summer. Put a fucking sign in the window saying: "Closed for summer holidays. Re-opening 1st September".'

'Impossible.'

'Ever been to the Canary Islands?'

'Yes, Barbara and I went to Lanzarote once.'

'Gran Canaria?'

'Nope.'

'Then I'll treat you! Let's sneak off to Las Palmas before wifey gets back. What d'you say?'

Look: I've told you, Eva, it's impossible. In any case, what on earth would I tell Barbara?'

'Oh, I don't know. Tell her you've been invited to speak at a book dealers' conference, or something.'

'Well for starters, secondhand book dealers don't DO conferences. We're all too impoverished. Thanks to the bloody charity shops!'

There was a long pause on the line (he suspected it was while a refill was being prepared). 'OK, I'll take that as a "maybe". Leave it with me and I'll get back to you with some dates.' Then there was a huge crash, followed by the sound of breaking glass. And the line went dead.

Anthony needed to put an end, once and for all, to the emotional turmoil of the last 18 hours and warn this crazy woman off. To nip things in the bud.

He locked the shop door and retired to the kitchenette to pen a letter to Eva, which he intended to post on his way home. It would leave her in no doubt that her 'cause' was a lost one.

*Kynaston Barn*
*Nr Ludlow*

*Dear Eva,*

*I must implore you to end this silly scheme of yours to try to re-start our old relationship. It ended six years ago. I am afraid you are living in the past if you believe that we can get together again.*

*Though we had some memorable times together (like Corsica), I have to confess that there were many unhappy incidents, which I would prefer to forget.*

*You are deluding yourself if you think that you can re-kindle a flame which has long since been extinguished.*

*I urge you - please desist.*

*Yours*
*Anthony*

He sealed the envelope and posted in the square on his way to collect the Fiat.

There was a big welcome from Ben when he arrived back at the barn just after 6.30p.m. As he took his little Sheltie out to stroll along the footpath for their evening walk, he was pleased to see the tidy manner in which the new gardener had begun to tackle the job of destroying the boundary hedge.

About half of the trench had already been excavated, with the space beneath carefully protected by strips of old plywood, held in place by bricks. He made a mental note to call the next morning at Williams, Ludlow's old-established ironmongers, to purchase the weed killer.

# IV

## *Cyril the Bookbinder*

ANTHONY HAD A FITFUL night alone in the barn, with a series of recurring anxiety dreams, brought on by his uncertainty about Eva's reaction to his letter. He awoke at 5.00a.m. and decided that that best thing to do was to get up and take Ben for a long walk. Dawn was breaking over Barnard's Wood as he set off, fortified by two cups of strong black coffee.

The tensions caused by Eva's mysterious reappearance – which he was now convinced was not a co-incidence – were not only getting to him, but were clearly affecting his relationship with Barbara. Before they had married, he had known that she wasn't the easiest person to get along with and, like many thespians, she would often over-dramatise situations.

By contrast, the placid book dealer was all for the quiet life, a life without constant incursions from the demanding Eva. But he wasn't sure whether the warning shot he had fired across her bows would deter her, or merely make her re-double her efforts.

Wednesdays were always busy market days in Ludlow and after opening the bookshop and checking his incoming postal orders, Anthony briefly nipped across for a chat with Terry, who was busily dressing his stall.

'We could be onto a winner with your Bradshaw, mate.'

'Really?'

'Yeah, there are some really fancy prices quoted on that world booksellers' internet site. I've arranged to call in to see Cyril my bookbinder on the way home tonight.'

'No hurries, mate.' Terry stopped laying out his array of bric-a-brac and looked across in the direction of the parade of shops where "Train Spotters" was located. 'Hey, are you planning to have your shopfront redecorated?'

'No, why?'

'There's a bird over there measuring your shop's doorway!'

Anthony looked across the square. He saw a bulky raincoated woman, stretching a measuring tape across the bottom of the shop's entrance door. 'Blimey, so there is. I'd better go and see what she wants.'

He marched purposefully over. 'Can I help you?'

The dumpy woman slowly stood up, checked him up and down rather quizzically and asked: 'Who are you?'

'What's more to the point: who are you and why are you measuring my door?'

She brought a thick pair of horn-rimmed spectacles up on a neck cord and perched them on the end of her beak-like nose, then consulted the blue plastic clipboard she was clutching in her other hand. 'Would you be Mr Anthony Metcalf?'

'What if I am? What business is it of yours?'

She turned the clipboard over and from a pouch handed him a visiting card. It read: "Pauline Campbell-Jones BSc Hons (Hobart). Disabled Access Compliance Officer." 'I take it you have received our formal notification?'

'You mean the five-page letter from the council which arrived yesterday? I'm afraid I've been too busy to study it in detail Mrs...'

'Mizz!' she hissed.

He checked the card. '... MISS Campbell-Jones.' Anthony unlocked the shop door and gestured for the woman to enter. 'Would you like to step inside and explain to me what's going on?'

'Certainly.'

After placing her clipboard and measuring tape on the counter, the council officer set forth on a tedious, jargon-filled narrative concerning Anthony's obligations to enlarge his shop's entrance, to enable wheelchair-users unhindered access. The word "deliver" was used frequently.

'But wheelchairs get in alright as it is.'

She peered at him sharply over the top of the spectacles' frame. 'Unaccompanied?'

'No. I grant you, there's usually someone pushing them, who helps get the wheels over the threshold.'

'That's not good enough, Mr Metcalf. The 2013 Act specifically requires un-assisted ingress.'

'Meaning?'

She exhaled with mock-exasperation, and consulted her clipboard, as if for reassurance. 'Meaning, Mr Metcalf: that your shop doorway must be widened. By at least twelve centimetres.' She pointed to the bottom of the door. 'And that projecting threshold must be removed.'

'Or?'

She glared. 'What do you mean 'or'?'

'What if I don't do it? What if I can't AFFORD to do it? What if I can't afford to have half of my shop front taken out – including two fragile old shop windows that probably haven't been disturbed for over a century?'

She shook her head. 'That's the law, Mr Metcalf.'

'And is the council planning to give me a grant – to recompense me for all this... upheaval? And Heaven knows what effect it will have on my trade.'

She adjusted her glasses, then dropped her eyelids. 'As to the council's grant-aided shop front funding scheme, I'm afraid that was withdrawn under the Treasury measures in the last Budget.' She paused before delivering her *coup-de-grace*. 'As to the... err...

consequences of non-compliance, then the authority would have no alternative but to carry out the necessary alterations itself.' The pen was slipped beneath the clipboard's chrome holder. 'And you would be billed for the work.'

'Catch 22.'

'I'm sorry?'

'A literary allusion, Mizz Campbell-Jones. Put rather more coarsely: damned if you do; damned if you don't.'

The Disabled Access Compliance Officer's response was another sniff. More of an equine snort this time.

He moved to the door and opened it. 'Now if you will excuse me, I've got work to do. I'm obliged to you for the explanation. Good morning.' Without responding, she swept out, her raincoat tails flapping.

Moments after he had slammed the door shut behind the official, Anthony's mobile pinged, signalling an incoming message. He knew it could only be from Eva.

"Ring me? I'm lonely! E x"

Realising his "warning shot" must now have passed across her bows, he slipped the phone back in his pocket and mused to himself: "Playing all pathetic now! That was invariably her reaction whenever we'd had had a scene. Best thing: let her stew for a bit!"

Sales were fairly brisk, partially cancelling out the morning's frustrations.

He packed three parcels for air-mailing to the United States and decided to get them over to the Post Office by noon, collecting a sandwich and a cappuccino on the way back. He paused, to regale Terry with the edited highlights of his encounter with his officious council visitor.

'Bloody superannuated jobsworths!' was the market trader's response. 'Oh, I meant to tell you: one of the stall holders was telling me this morning that the new British steam loco *Tornado* is coming through Ludlow next week. Had you heard?'

'No, when?'

'Saturday 5th September. Could be a great opportunity for your bookshop, mate.'

'How so?'

'Well according the excursion's timetable, the new train's going to be here for three hours.'

'That's probably because they're all foodies. Don't forget, it's the final day of the Ludlow Food Festival.'

'But they're train spotters too; rich train spotters. You don't get much change from £100 when you go on one of them special excursions, you know? Check out the itinerary when you get back to your shop, pal. It could be a real boost for your sales.'

'Thanks Terry, I might just do that. What I really came over to tell you – before that bitch in the blue raincoat turned up - was that I'm going to see Cyril my bookbinder on the way home tonight. To show him the Bradshaw. I'll let you know what he says. Right, I'd better get back.'

He crossed the cobbled square and headed for his shop. As he passed the town's old Assembly Rooms building, he heard the staccato rasp of a high-performance sports car, as it ascended Mill Street from the direction of the River Teme. It was travelling fast – well above the speed limit. And he was certain it was a Porsche. Surely not a visit from an irate Eva?

Frantically, he ducked into the Assembly Rooms' box office and peered through the glass entrance doors - just as yellow blur streaked by. He breathed a sigh of relief: it was a modern Boxster, with some grinning half-wit at the wheel showing off to his girlfriend. He strolled quietly back to "Train Spotters".

While the shop was empty, Anthony rang Jack Nugent, the father of the young man who had come to his assistance at the fete car park. Jack told Anthony that his son was away at an army cadet camp.

'He's really keen on the army life, your lad, isn't he?'

'You bet. Plans to join the Royal Engineers – provided he can get the required grades in his exams. He wants to be a combat engineer.'

'When's he back from camp?'

'Friday evening.'

'Could you ask him to give me a call at home, Jack? I've got a little Saturday job that might interest him. I'll give him some pocket money.'

'I'll get Tim to ring you, Anthony. I'm sure he'll be glad to help.'

Reaching under the counter to withdraw the plastic carrier containing the Bradshaw he was taking to the bookbinder, Anthony brushed against Eva's jiffy bag. He took it to the kitchenette and deposited it in the rubbish bin.

Caynham was less than five miles south-east of the town. It was a pretty drive, with the B-road running alongside a small river which flowed towards Tenbury Wells. The Mumfords' cottage was set on its own at the end of the village.

Anthony sauntered down through the cottage garden. The bookbinder's workshop was at the far end of the lawn. Its close-boarded timber exterior was finished in a pale blue, with the small casements picked out in jade green, each with a pair of cream shutters. It had a roof of moss-covered cedar shingles. Above the central door was a hand-painted sign announcing: "C. MUMFORD ~ PRINTING & BOOKBINDING". It looked, for all the world, like a well-preserved Arts & Crafts cricket pavilion. Anthony tapped on the door and entered.

The well-lit rectangular space was tidy and ordered. Along the far wall was a wide window overlooking a small spinney, through which a brook ran. Suspended by brass chains from the workshop's sloping ceiling was a wide-screen TV, showing a cricket match in progress. The bookbinder reached across to a remote control and muted the commentary.

'Afternoon, Cyril.'

'Come on in Anthony,' the old man murmured, without looking up. 'Take a seat.'

'How are we doing?'

'The Test? We're annihilating 'em. Just let me finish this titling, will you?'

'Sure.' Anthony set the carrier bag containing Terry's Bradshaw on the floor and watched the cricket match.

Dressed in a blue denim shirt and jeans and a maroon apron, the rotund bookbinder was perched on a stool, finishing the gold embossing on the spine of an old bible, which was held in front of him in a vice. He balanced a small book of gold leaf on one knee. The all-pervading aroma in the workshop was a pleasing mixture of new leather and old paper.

In front of the big window was a 2m-deep working surface of varnished plywood. Along the left-hand wall of the workshop were ply-formed racks containing bundles of buckram bookcloth and various leather bindings, from morocco to calf and pigskin. A label on an old plan chest indicated that its contents were backing boards and marbled paper. The opposing side wall was a veritable cornucopia of bookbinding tools, all neatly stored in labelled slots. There were fillet wheels, polishing irons and rows of old wooden-handled patterning tools. Trays of type were slotted below.

Pride of place on the workbench was given to a decorated Victorian pinch press, with its two gilded cast-iron arms sweeping up to terminate beneath a three-pronged central wheel. Paste tubs and brushes were set beside a single gas ring at the corner of the workbench, with a well-worn oilstone alongside. Several steel type rules and pairs of callipers hung from hooks on the wall.

The old man stroked an index finger across his brow then wiped it onto the top of the gold leaf pad, causing the first sheet to adhere to his fingertip. Holding it above the book's spine, he gave a gentle puff to blow it onto the leather. Then he carefully reached across to select a brass-ended patterning tool, which he slowly impressed onto the gold leaf. He paused for a moment, laid down the tool and placed the golf leaf pad on the workbench.

He leaned back and gave Anthony a cheerful smile. 'Right, I'll leave that to set. Now let's see what you've brought me, shall we?'

Cyril Mumford gingerly withdrew the Bradshaw from its bag and placed it on the workbench. 'Dear me – this has seen better days, hasn't it?' The bookbinder then began a forensic examination of the Victorian railway timetable.

'Back board's gone.' He ran his finger over the decorated paper opposite. 'I'm pretty sure we've got a marbled endpaper which will match this. It's never lost its popularity. Now what have we got here at the front? I say – see this?' He tapped a decorated rectangular plate affixed to the marbled endpaper inside the front cover board. On it were several lines of ornate copperplate script.

'What is it, Cyril?'

'Seems to be a dedication panel. Looks as if this was a special edition of that year's Bradshaw, made as a presentation. He read out the wording on the label. '"Presented to Sir Gilbert Okle, on the occasion of his retirement from the Board of Directors of the Shrewsbury to Hereford Railway Company. October 1896." Nice little addition, that.'

'Really?'

'Oh yes. Gives it authenticity; makes it a cut above your run-of-the-mill Bradshaw.'

He flipped the volume over and slowly ran an index finger around the curved decoration on the front cover. 'Blind embossed cloverleaf. Very tidy. Yes, we've got that pattern. It'll need thick mill board to give the depth. He turned the book on edge and squinted at the shabby state of the spine. Only a few small remnants of calf skin clung to the webbed linen cloth.

'I think it wants a ribbed spine. And for your gilded title – which is missing - I'm pretty sure they'd have used Baskerville. Which we've got.'

'Is it old?'

'Older than your Bradshaw. By a good century. Lucky that dedicated front end paper's intact, eh? That's what's going to give it some value, Anthony. If I was you, I'd put a note on your internet advert saying that the back board is an authentic replica. That way you won't get any come-backs from collectors, who could claim they'd been duped. If you get my meaning?'

'Oh, absolutely. I think that's very sensible. So what would it all cost – the restoration you've just outlined?'

Cyril Mumford reached across for a scrap of paper and jotted some figures down with a pencil, which he took from behind his ear. He slid the paper away and rocked his head slowly back and forth. 'How does £75 sound to you? Plus the dreaded VAT, of course.'

'It sounds more than reasonable, Cyril. Let me have a word with my partner, will you? I'll try to get back to you with a decision before the weekend, if that's OK?'

'Fine. It's a bit quiet at the moment, so I could probably make a start on it - if you decide to go ahead - towards the end of the month.'

The two men talked on for a while, mostly reminiscing about their respective cricketing heroes. They agreed that Ian Botham had been the last of the true cricketing buccaneers.

The old bookbinder gazed fondly out of the window to the spinney below. 'Mind you, a fine David Gower cover drive was something to behold.' He chuckled and patted his ample stomach. 'I remember seeing him play at a charity match down at Berrington Hall once. He broke three car windscreens, with successive sixes!'

Anthony excused himself, saying he had to get back to feed and walk the dog.

On his way through Kynaston village, Anthony saw that the lights were on in St Guthrac's Church, indicating the usual Wednesday evening choir practice, which Barbara usually attended. The Redknapps' black Mercedes limo was parked by the lychgate.

The answerphone was signalling a stored message when he arrived home. Would it be Barbara or Eva? He poured himself a large glass of wine.

"Anthony? I've tried reaching you at the shop and at the barn," announced an obviously irked Barbara on the recording. "Ring me on my mobile will you? I need to tell you about a change of plan. And don't make it too late please, as I have to be up before six tomorrow." He called her immediately.

'I couldn't get hold of you. Where were you?'

'I called in to see Cyril Mumford, the bookbinder. I've only just walked through the door.'

'I see.' The response had a hint of suspicion about it. 'Well, all being well, we'll be finished tomorrow because they need to strike the set for another production. I thought as it's going to be pretty late - and I expect we'll all go somewhere for supper – I'd ring Stephenie and ask if I could stay with her at the flat in Primrose Hill.'

'And drive back on Friday?'

'Yes, probably.'

'Fine by me, Barbara. Just give me a bit of notice when you'll be back as our food stocks are a bit on the low side.'

'Everything OK at the shop?'

'So-so. I've known better weeks, I must say. And being cross-examined this morning by the council's Disabled Access Compliance Officer didn't exactly make my day.'

'Disabled what?'

'I'll save the lurid details until you get back. It's just another problem I could do without, right now.'

'OK. You can tell me about it at the weekend.'

'I will. Goodnight.'

# V

## *Legal Advice*

THERE REMAINED an ominous, brooding silence from Eva. It was fully twenty-four hours since they had spoken, and in all probability she would have no recollection of the conversation.

Anthony was just preparing to drive into Ludlow to open the shop when the house phone rang. It was an early morning call from Barbara.

'I thought I'd catch you before you left as we're going to be tied up on the set virtually all day. I spoke to Steph last night and there's some great news.'

'What's that?'

'Well, she says it's fine for me to stay with her, but on Saturday night she's due to attend the London premiere of the film she's been working on: *"Gambit 2"*. It's the sequel to *"Gambit"*. The one the Coen brothers scripted.'

'I vaguely remember it. About forged artworks?'

'That's it. She did it after the Harry Potter series finished. Well she's got a spare ticket for the premiere and wants me to go with her! It's at the Odeon Leicester Square.'

'Lucky you! What will you wear?'

'Oh I'll wear one of Steph's dresses as we're roughly the same size. So if it's all the same to you, I won't be driving back now until Sunday.'

'You go and enjoy yourself, Barbara. You've earned it, with the long hours you've done this week. And give Steph my love.'

Anthony parked in a supermarket car park at the bottom of the town, in order to make a call at Williams, the old-established ironmongers.

'Good morning, Mr Metcalf. How are you today, sir?' asked an elderly assistant, who was storing brass screws in a small wooden storage drawer.

'Fine thank you, Harold. And yourself?'

'Fair to middling. The legs playing up a bit, sir, but otherwise fine.' He slid the labelled drawer into a wall-mounted storage cabinet of some fifty or so identical drawers. 'What can we get you this morning?'

'I'd like a can of weed killer, please. The strongest you've got.'

'What sort of weeds are you eradicating, Mr Metcalf?'

Anthony chose his words carefully. 'A virulent evergreen shrub.'

The old man moved down the counter and slid a small step ladder under a row of high shelves. One step at a time, he cautiously ascended until he was within arm's reach of a row of tin cans. He gingerly withdrew a white can and brought it down, placing it on the counter in front of Anthony.

'There you are, Mr Metcalf – that's the one you want.' He angled it, to study the small print on the side of the can. 'Glyphosate: that's the active ingredient that does all the damage. This one's a super-concentrate: 350 grammes per litre. It's the strongest we sell. I should be sure to keep it out of harm's way.'

'I certainly will. All right if I pay with plastic?' Anthony enquired, fishing out his wallet.

'Certainly sir. I'll just get the gadget. Won't be a moment.'

Having purchased the weed killer for the new gardener, Anthony collected the Fiat and parked it in its usual space behind the square. The weather was set fair and it promised to be a busy shopping day in Ludlow.

After the first phase of customers had been and gone, he put in a call to his solicitors, who were located close by. After a pause, he was connected to junior partner, Gerald Stewart.

'Anthony – how are you? Long time no see.'

'I know, Gerald, it's been quite a while, hasn't it?'

'Barbara OK?'

'Yes, she's fine. Away filming at the moment.'

'"Hotel Majestic"? We both watch it every Sunday tell her. So, what can I do for you this morning?'

'I received a rather complicated document from the council earlier in the week, followed up yesterday by a visit from a most officious woman.'

'What's the document about?'

'Disabled access, as far as I can make out. But it's all couched in such obscure bureaucratic gobbledegook that it's hard to make head or tail of it. And talking to her – this woman council officer – didn't throw much more light on the subject. I was wondering if I could pop round and show it to you.'

'Of course. Better still, why not drop it into reception today, I'll peruse it overnight, and then you could drop by tomorrow for a chat? It'll save us both time.'

'Good idea.'

'Right, just let me check my Friday appointments.' After a pause, the solicitor returned to the line. '11.30a.m. tomorrow any good for you?'

'Yes, that would be fine. I'll drop the letter into reception at lunchtime and then call by to see you tomorrow.'

There had been no communication from Eva in the morning's post at the shop, nor had she rung or sent any text messages. The silence was becoming ominous. Sipping his tea in the back kitchenette, Anthony reflected that his "please desist" letter may have been unduly harsh. He began to feel a bit of a heel. He remembered of old that when this woman went into her shell after being scolded, she would sometimes not emerge for several days.

An analysis of the shop's weekly till roll revealed that book sales had been surprisingly buoyant, boosted by the Russian window display. He retrieved some more of the old tramp's postcards from the store room, intending to ask Tim Nugent to create a special display of them at the back of the counter, if he came in to work in the shop on the Saturday.

The next visitor to "Train Spotters" was Terry and Anthony gave him a potted report of Cyril Mumford's findings.

'Did you tell him to go ahead?'

'I said I'd consult you, then I'd ring him.'

'Let's give it a go, shall we? After all, ninety quid ain't a huge outlay. And who knows, done up it might fetch £200-250. Want to go 50:50?'

'If you're happy. OK, I'll ring Cyril this afternoon and give him the go-ahead.'

'Thanks mate.' Terry left to return to his unattended stall and Anthony resumed his accounting. In his lunch break, he dashed round to the solicitors to leave the council's document for Gerald Stewart to mull over.

Eva finally emerged from her shell on Thursday afternoon. Far from being hostile or even truculent, she was subdued, even chastened.

'So where are you? At the cottage?'

'Yes.'

'Sun-bathing?'

'No reading, actually. Tolstoy.'

'Looking forward to Sunday?'

'Not really.'

'Why?'

'Oh, you know: last-minute nerves. It's not every weekend that a girl has to tackle an international hill climb run in front of a crowd of several thousands.'

'I'm sure. It's mighty plucky of you to go in for it.'

'Apparently it's going to be televised.'

'Really? Which channel?'

'Not sure. I'll text you when I get there.' There was a pause on the line, as if she hadn't quite finished the sentence. 'Sure you don't want to come?'

'That's very kind of you, Eva, but... I'm really committed to doing the shop's stock take. The accountants are screaming for it for my tax return,' he lied.

'Of course.' Eva's submission, he thought, was out of character. A catty riposte was the norm. After a pause, she started gently fishing. 'Wifey still away filming?'

'Barbara's returning Saturday night or Sunday morning. She's been invited by an old friend to attend a film premiere in London.'

Had Eva's sexual antenna been switched on, Anthony wondered. 'Nice. So... you're going to be home alone for two more nights?'

'Seems so.'

'Poor you. And surviving on sardines-on-toast, I imagine?' (How did this woman know that the pantry was practically bare?)

'A bit more imaginative than that, Eva. But, yes, we're on subsistence rations at the moment.'

'"We?"'

'Me and Ben; my Sheltie whom you've not met.'

After a long silence: 'Anthony?'

'Yes, Eva?'

'I do so want to see you, darling.' She really sounded close to tears. 'Not in your bloody shop or in a down-at-heel restaurant. I want us to be able to spend some time together again. Quality time. Like it used to be. Don't you remember how it used to be?'

He couldn't withhold the admission. 'Of course I do.'

'All right for you to talk?' she enquired, as if sensing his edginess.

'Yeah, fine at the moment. I may have to break off if we get a customer.' It was the usual 1.00-2.00p.m. lull and the shop remained deserted.

There was another long pause on the line. No drinking seemed to be involved, although he could clearly check the pace of her breathing.

'Come round tonight, sweetest? Pleaaaaase? Let me cook you one of my wonderful suppers? Like I used to? What do you say?'

What, indeed, does one say to an offer like that? From such a seductively beautiful mature woman? A woman who is making it abundantly clear that the *cordon bleu* dinner she wants to prepare for you will almost certainly be followed by a night of *cordon bleu* sex.

She allowed the seconds to tick for him to take in the full implications of the invitation.

'Anthony?'

'Yes, I'm still here.'

'Darling, you're going be home all alone tonight. I am too. It's crazy! Why shouldn't we... enjoy it?'

'Enjoy what exactly?'

'Enjoy... this... reunion. Us meeting again.'

'Eva... honestly, I simply can't...'

More seconds ticked by, synchronised by her slow, methodical breathing.

Callously, he switched to middle-aged, married man mode. 'I'm sorry. It's quite impossible.'

The ding of the shop door rang, like the end of a boxing round in which the two participants had merely paced around the ring. Saved by the bell. He poked his head out from the kitchen.

'Got any old GWR timetables? Pre-1940?'

Hurriedly (but relieved) he told her: 'Sorry. Got a customer. Must go.'

After composing himself, Anthony told the insignificant male customer: 'They're down here at the back. Beyond the DVDs.'

The man eventually found three soiled timetables, for which he happily paid £3 and left the shop.

The afternoon dragged on. There were no more calls from Eva.

It was 4.45p.m and everything had gone quiet. Turning off the lights in the back kitchen area, Anthony prepared to leave. But his mobile phone intended him to remain.

"Ping". The incoming text message read: "WHAT TIME SHALL I EXPECT YOU?"

He moved to the front of the shop and locked the door, then returned to the kitchenette. He rang Eva, who answered immediately.

'Eva, I thought I made it clear at lunchtime, I won't be coming over this evening.' Silence. 'Are you there?'

'Yes. But I'm very hurt. I think you're being SO unreasonable.'

'Look, Eva, I told you in my note that it's a pointless exercise you've embarked on... to try to... start up something that finished a long time ago. Six years ago.'

'It may be six years, but it hasn't altered how I feel about you. Please say you'll come?'

Now it was he who decided to use the weapon of silence.

'Anthony? Are you there?'

'I was just on the point of leaving the shop, actually. I really must get home to feed the dog. He's been locked inside all day.'

'Well if you won't come over, will you ring me later?'

'I'll see.'

There followed another long pause. 'How would it be if we... you know, if we tried something naughty?'

'Naughty?'

'Phone sex?'

'Oh come off it!'

'Remember how we used to do it? You were hot stuff in those days. Pleaaaase? For old time's sake? Might set me up nicely for the hill climb on Sunday. You never know, I might even break the course record!'

He felt uncomfortable now. 'Look I'd better go. I'll try to call you later. After I've walked Ben.'

She ended with a seductive sing-song whisper. 'I'll be waiting!'

Anthony watched the BBC's six o'clock news bulletin while feeding the dog. He stuck a prepared supermarket meal in the microwave, but only picked at it. He wanted to get out and walk before it got dark. Walking seemed to settle him when he was agitated. Before setting off across the field to Barnard's Wood, he stored the can of weed killer on the shelf in the garage, ready for the gardener to use.

The old grandfather clock was chiming 8.00p.m. as he let himself back into the barn and saw the warning light on his mobile phone was signalling that an incoming text message had arrived. It could only be from one person.

He opened it: "READY AND WAITING EAGERLY FOR YOUR CALL. E xxx". He just couldn't bring himself to make it – and certainly didn't want to contemplate what it might lead to. Then a second text arrived: "WHERE ARE YOU?" He tapped in her number.

'Anthony! At last – I was beginning to think you'd stood me up. Can we begin?'

'Eva: let's be adult about this, shall we?'

'What are you talking about, darling?'

'What am I talking about? You know very well what I'm talking about. I'm talking about this cat-and-mouse game you seem to be playing with a happily married man. A married man who has no intention of being unfaithful to his wife, either in your bed or over the bloody phone! THAT'S what I'm taking about!'

Her breathing was heavy and indicated her resentment at this severe dressing down. 'I see. I might as well have an early night, then.' The line went dead and he recalled how often, in the past, Eva had played the pouting, chastened little girl card. At that moment, he was pretty certain she would be heading for the bottle on the sideboard marked: "REMY MARTIN VSOP".

Anthony was about to go up to bed when the house phone went. He was relieved that it was only Tim Nugent, calling after returning from cadet camp.

'Thanks for ringing, Tim, How was camp?'

'Great. I really enjoyed it. I learned a lot as well.'

'Good. Look, I was wondering how you'd feel about coming and helping me out at the shop on Saturday? Just a half-day, maybe? In the afternoon?'

'Sure. I'd be happy to. So long as you show me how to operate the till!'

'Of course. And I'll explain all the stock we've got. And if we're not too busy, I'd like to go over an idea I've got for a little bit of marketing to boost sales at "Train Spotters."'

'Fine. Be glad to help. I'll probably cycle in. Would two o'clock be OK?'

'Excellent. I'll see you on Saturday then.'

'Goodnight.'


On the Friday morning, Anthony locked the shop up just before 11.30a.m., flipped the plywood loco sign over and walked down to his solicitors' office in Mill Street. It was one of Ludlow's finest half-timbered houses, with its outside rendering now decorated in a distinctive hue of mustard yellow between the creosoted oak beams.

He was ushered into Gerald Stewart's office at the back of the ground floor. The middle-aged solicitor, in an open-necked check shirt, rose to greet him. His head was clean-shaven.

'Come on in, Anthony.'

The visitor stared at the shiny cranium. Gerald stroked his hand across it. 'You obviously don't approve.'

'No I do not! Whatever made you do that?'

'Oh you know – widow's peek and a bald patch at the back. Celia persuaded me to have it all off.'

'One of my three trendy urban living phobias.'

'The other two being?

'Personalised number plates and women with tattooed arms.'

'Guilty as charged on two of the three counts, Your Honour, I'm afraid.'

'Don't tell me your wife has had her arms tattooed, Gerald?'

'No, but she's got her name plastered across the front of her 4x4. Anyway, have a seat.'

The solicitor had the council's letter in front of him on his desk. He tapped the first page. 'Bit of a facer this one, isn't it? And you say you also had a visit?'

Anthony extracted the council officer's card from his top pocket and passed it across the desk. 'Yes. From a Miss Pauline Campbell-Jones, Disabled Access Compliance Officer. A right battleaxe. I'm afraid we had words.'

'Oh dear.' He picked up the letter. 'This is the first one of these I've seen, but I'd heard about them at Rotary. Several colleagues in other practices in the town have had the same thing.'

'So what's going on?'

'In a nutshell: the government has been coming under pressure from the major disabled charities to improve disabled access in public buildings, supermarkets, shops and so on. So they, in turn, put pressure on local authorities via ministerial directives; who, in turn, put pressure on the poor old shopkeepers. Which is why you're in the firing line.'

'Do I have any redress? It's going to cost me an arm and a leg to alter my shop front. Several thousands, I expect. And that woman told me there are no grants available.'

'Redress? You mean appeal? I'm afraid not. It's part of an Act of Parliament. They're pretty relentless, too. You know the big supermarket at the bottom of the town?'

'Where the cattle market used to be?'

'That's the one. Well when it was being built, it was discovered that there was going to be a height difference of just under one metre between the pavement and the supermarket's shop floor. The council made them insert a long disabled ramp, with a gradient sufficiently shallow for a wheelchair user to propel himself up it unaided. It's all of 12 metres long. You take a look at it. By comparison, your front doorstep's a mere pin-prick.

'I hate to sound like Rumpole, but to be honest, you haven't got a leg to stand on, old man. They've got you all ways up. This document (he waved the 5-page letter in the air) probably took a middle-ranking council officer a week to compose. It'll be watertight, believe you me.'

'So what you're saying is: "You might as well get the alterations carried out, or face the consequences of enforcement"?'

'In a word, yes.'

'How long have I got?'

'Well these people don't exactly move at the speed of light.' He studied the officer's visiting card before handing it back. 'But in view of your brush with this woman, I think we can assume that she'll be keeping an eye out for signs of the building work being started. I'd get it done by the end of the year, if I was you.'

Glumly, Anthony responded: 'Then I suppose I'd better get some quotes.'

'Is your frontage listed?'

'No.'

'Well that's a bonus; one less council official you'll have to satisfy.'

'But all the half-decent builders in this town seem to be pretty busy. They're not going to come cheap, these alterations, you know? I can't afford to entrust it to bodgers. I guess I'm going to have to apply for a short-term bank loan.'

The solicitor leaned back in his plush executive office chair.

'We're having some work done out at our place at the moment. We're extending the garage and adding an attic space as a games room for the kids. The builders who are doing it seem extremely competent, especially the chippies. Would you like me to have a word with the boss to see whether he'd be willing to tackle your shopfront?'

'Would you, Gerald?'

'Certainly. I'll give him a call at the site after you've gone and get him to give you a ring. His name is Jack Edwards.'

'I'd really appreciate it.'

Anthony glanced at the antique carriage clock on the mantelpiece. 'I'd better be getting back to the shop. Thanks for you time, Gerald.' The session had lasted less than half-an-hour.

'Good to see you, again Anthony. Do give my regards to Barbara.'


Promptly at 1.30p.m.on Saturday, Tim Nugent arrived at "Train Spotters". He was in full cycling gear and helmet, pushing a spotless yellow mountain bike.

'I'm a bit early, because I need to change and grab this sandwich I've brought, if that's OK?'

The proprietor ushered the youth through to the back of the shop, storing his bike in the passage. 'Come up to the till area at 2.00p.m., after you've had your lunch, and I'll show you the ropes.'

Anthony and Tim got on well from the outset, the young man was quick to pick up details and eager to become involved in the shop's operations. He seemed to have no problems mastering the till or the credit card terminal.

When there was a brief lull, Anthony asked: 'Right: tell me – are you up to speed on *Tornado*?'

Tim reflected for a moment. 'Well, it's a built-from-scratch loco – so it wasn't a restoration. It's Peppercorn Class. I can't remember its number; six hundred something, I think. It was funded by steam enthusiasts without any government help and it's said to be the first brand new steam locomotive to be built in the UK for half a century. But I've never actually seen it.'

Anthony gave a big smile. 'Not bad. Not bad at all. 6013 is its number.' He nodded towards the book shelves. 'Jonathan Glancey's history of the project down there sells reasonably well, so you can mug up some other facts and figures if we're quiet this afternoon. The big news is that *Tornado* is coming to Ludlow. So you'll be able to see it for yourself next Saturday!"

'Wow!'

'Wow, indeed. Which is why we need to get all the train enthusiasts who'll be riding in its Pullman cars up here and browsing in "Train Spotters"!

'And you want me to help?'

'If you're willing'?

The two *Tornado* fans then got their heads together to discuss the details of Anthony's marketing wheeze. This was to print off an A5 flyer, which Tim would hand out on Ludlow Station platform as the excursion's passengers got off the train. The boy was red-hot on logistics.

'These special excursions normally have eight Pullmans. Eight carriages; ten compartments; six to a compartment. So that's 480, if it's sold out.'

'Which it almost certainly will be.'

'Let's do a print run of 500, shall we?' the boy suggested.

Now feeling very much happier about his plan to boost his shop's sales, Anthony told Tim Nugent he needed to nip out to buy some flowers for Barbara's home-coming.

'You sure you'll be OK here on your own?'

'No probs, Mr Metcalf. Take as long as you like.'

'I'll be back by 4.00p.m. And call me Anthony.'

Anthony headed for the pedestrian passage at the top of Corve Street, which connects with the town's modern civic library. The passageway in front of the florists was bursting with summer blooms. Ten minutes later, as he emerged with an armful of flowers, he bumped into Doris Redknapp.

'Your friend not with you today, Mr Metcalf?'

Mrs Rednapp was the sort of two-faced gossip who would courteously use "your friend" to Anthony's face, but an epithet like "fancy woman" or "trollop" behind his back, to the ladies of the local bridge circle.

'No, Mrs Redknapp. I haven't seen her since the fete last Sunday.'

'Really? One of my neighbours said they saw her today, driving through town in that little sports car of hers.'

His heart sank. Surely Eva wasn't planning another of her theatrical appearances at his shop? As it turned out (he was soon to be regaled about it by an amused Tim Nugent), Eva had been and gone.

Anthony excused himself from the old gossip and hurried back. 'Everything OK?' he asked as he slipped back into the shop.

'Yup. Been pretty hectic, though. I sold 20 of your Russian postcards; one customer bought all the ones of the *SS Baikal*. By the way, you had a visitor.'

After storing the flowers in water in the kitchenette, Anthony joined his new assistant at the counter. 'A visitor, you say?'

'The lady you were at Codrington Manor with last Sunday. She was looking for you. But unfortunately she got into a bit of an altercation with one of the town's parking officers.'

'Oh yes?' Anthony knew what was coming next.

'She'd only just stepped through the door and this rather officious bloke came in and gave her a ticket because she'd left her Porsche on a double yellow line. It caused quite a commotion.'

'What happened?'

'She tore it up in front of him, called him a fascist pig, stormed out of the shop and drove off at high speed.'

'Blimey.'

'The customers in the shop thought it was a hoot.'

Doubtless stung by her brush with the authorities, Eva didn't put in another appearance at "Train Spotters", though Anthony suspected that he would be given a first hand account by phone later.

Anthony and Tim worked in tandem for the rest of the afternoon and eventually closed up at 6.00p.m. Anthony handed the boy a £20 note and thanked him warmly. As he wheeled out his mountain bike, Tim called out: 'Let me know when you've got those flyers printed, Anthony? I'll come in early next Saturday to pick them up, then cycle down to the station. *Tornado's* due in at 10.15a.m.'

'Thanks again, Tim. You've been a terrific help.'

'I really enjoyed it.'

Anthony was pleased his frantic working week was ended. He intended to have an early night and certainly wasn't going to be beguiled by the siren of Bishop's Frome.

As he was preparing Ben's food, his mobile phone pinged. 'Bang on cue, Eva,' thought Anthony to himself as he placed the dog bowl on the tiled floor. He switched off the phone without even bothering to read the text.

# VI

## *Shelsley Walsh*

---

BEFORE RETIRING, Anthony had forgotten to pull the big bedroom curtains. In consequence, he was awoken before 6.00a.m. by dazzling shafts of morning sunshine streaming across the bed. He wasn't sorry to be disturbed, as his slumbers had been a series of endless re-runs of bawdy romps with Eva, across deserted Corsican beaches.

Half-awake, he hazily remembered that it was this morning that he had set aside to complete the digging of the garden trench behind the doomed Leylandii. And to prepare a special Sunday supper for Barbara's homecoming.

He sat at the kitchen table with a mug of strong tea and idly switched on his mobile phone – not so much out of curiosity, as in preparation for a message or call from Barbara, alerting him to the time of her return in the evening. But the only message was the one from Eva the previous evening: "IF WE CAN'T BE TOGETHER IN MY BED TONIGHT, LET'S MAKE LOVE ON THE PHONE! E xxx"

Anthony donned his gardening jeans and Wellington boots and carried the tools out from the garage. It was already getting warm and the long-haired Sheltie sensibly lay inside the garage in the shade. After setting aside the boards and bricks, Anthony made short work of taking out the remaining section of the trench. He spiked the V-shaped bottom with a fork, in preparation for the first application of the weed killer, but then decided to make himself a coffee.

As he went back into the kitchen (shadowed by Ben), his phone pinged. The incoming message simply read: "I'M ON TV NOW! CHANNEL 6. E x". It was just before noon. He reached over and clicked the remote control, to bring up a picture on the kitchen's TV

"... at the famous Shelsley Walsh hill climb here in Worcestershire. And you join us at a most fascinating moment – perhaps even unprecedented, Sir Andrew?"

"Indeed. I've certainly never seen this happen before, in all the years I've been coming here."

"And how long is that?"

"I'd rather not say!"

"Too modest, Sir Andrew – but at least four decades, I dare say! Well viewers, what you see on your screens now is the two lady drivers who have just put in identical times to tie for first place in the Ladies' All-Comers Contest for the coveted Baxendale Trophy. They've just returned to the paddock and are awaiting an official ruling. Both runs were done in a blistering 30.04 seconds. And in case you're not familiar with times here at Shelsley, that's only six-and-a-half seconds behind the women's all-time best. What's more, that record was set in a four-litre single-seater racing car!

"On the left of your screen you see the magnificent British Racing Green D-type Jaguar, with its owner, Shelsley Walsh veteran, the French driver Pénélopie Garnier." The camera shot showed a very large lady in grease-smeared white overalls, conferring with her three male mechanics, all wearing blue overalls.

"And on the right of the screen, you can see the diminutive 1955 Porsche Spyder of novice Mrs Eva Carlssen, who is standing beside it." Eva was talking to a broad-shouldered woman in a brown cloche hat. "I say 'novice' but, more correctly, I should really say 'Shelsley Walsh newcomer'. Because she drove that Porsche beautifully, didn't she Andrew?"

"A faultless run, Tom, with real panache."

"Ever driven one?"

"As a matter of fact, I have. At the Nurburgring. On the old circuit. It was after a 12-hour sports car race there, in which Spyders took the first three places. Jo Bonnier let me take his car round the circuit once. And as a circuit of the old Ring in those days was nearly thirteen miles it was quite a drive, I can tell you."

"Exciting?"

"Breathtaking. The power-to-weight ratio was near-perfect – so well-balanced – the handling was precise, and because it's so low-slung, with its 1500-litre power unit literally sat behind your shoulder blades, it sticks to the road like a limpet. If she owns that car we're looking at, Mrs Carlssen is a very lucky woman."

"What would you say it's worth?"

"Well there were only 90 of them which ever came out of the Stuttgart works, so they're very rare. Assuming that that's an original – which I'm pretty sure it is – I'd guess it's got to be worth around £2-million. I can tell you that earlier this year, a later derivative - the RS61 - was sold in London for £1.9-million. That one was owned by Sir Stirling Moss."

"Who is here at Shelsley today!"

"Indeed. The thing that is utterly unique about the Spyder is that it's a sports racing car which the owner can drive to the circuit. I happen to know that Mrs Carlssen drove that little car here this morning."

Eva was shown dressed in crisp white culottes over silver baseball boots, with a body-hugging open-weave silver silk blouse, with a wide red leather belt. In one hand she held a silver crash helmet and in the other her long snakeskin driving gloves. She looked calm, relaxed and very beautiful.

"On your screen now viewers, while we await the Race Marshal's ruling on the two ladies' identical timings, you can see Derek Bell – there on the left, in his distinctive racing overalls – with Stirling

Moss, still looking sprightly at 85, alongside him. They're signing autographs in the entrance of the old barn. And that fearsome white monster that's parked in front of them, is the 635 brake horsepower Porsche 956 which Derek drove in the 1963 season."

"And to put that bhp figure in context Tom, that's equivalent to eight family Fiestas! For my money, Derek Bell is the greatest Englishman ever to compete in endurance motor racing: five Le Mans wins and three Daytonas."

"Agreed. What about Sir Stirling, Andrew? What would you say was his greatest achievement?"

"Unquestionably the 1955 Mille Miglia road race which sadly no longer takes place, having been banned by the Pope in 1957. Moss, and his navigator Denis Jenkinson, completed the one thousand mile round-Italy circuit at a staggering average speed of 97.96 mph. Just imagine that: maintaining an average speed of almost one hundred miles an hour over one thousand kilometres of ordinary public roads."

"Awesome. What were they driving?"

"A Mercedes. It looked like a streamlined two-seater sports racing car, but it was, to all intents and purposes, a 250-brake-horse power Formula one racing car, disguised as a road car."

The TV picture Anthony was watching now showed the two women drivers being spoken to by an official wearing a deerstalker hat and a tweed jacket, bearing a huge rosette on its lapel.

"So what's going on down there in the paddock, Andrew?"

"Well, I'd say that the Race Marshal we can see talking to the two ladies – that's Major Brian Low - is offering them the choice of splitting the prize money – that's a cheque for £1000 and a magnum of champagne – or having a run-off. And as he's getting a coin out of his jacket pocket, it looks as if they're going to toss for a run-off. How exciting!"

The marshal spun the coin high into the air and the two women watched it fall onto the tarmac. The three figures stared down at the coin. The Race Marshal looked expectantly towards Eva, who smiled and nodded.

"Well it looks like Mrs Carlssen made a successful call and she's opted for a sudden death run-off. I'm sure she'll want to go up first."

"Who's your money on?"

"I'm going to go with the Spyder, Tom. Not only because of Mrs Carlssen's first run, which was simply superb; a textbook exercise in how to go up Shelsley. But because, as I've said, that little Porsche hugs the road, making it ideal for the subtle twists and turns here. Whereas, Penny Garnier's Jag – by the way, this one was driven at Le Mans by Mike Hawthorn in 1955 – is a brute of a machine to keep in check on a tight hill climb. There's three-and-a-half litres under that long front bonnet, and at over three-quarters of a ton, it weighs half as much again as the little Spyder."

The TV camera panned up from the crowded paddock scene to show the lower section of the hill climb circuit, snaking up under a canopy of tall conifers and then curving away to the left-hand edge of the screen. A crowd of more than 500 were seated in the shade of the terraced grandstand.

"Well the red flags are out, which means that the last batch of lady drivers will be coming back down the hill from the finish line. Here they are now: a brace of Cooper Nortons there, followed by a trusty old Morgan three-wheeler – an original 1932 "Moggy", that one. That's followed by a gaggle of Austin Healey Sprites and then bringing up the rear is Miss Scarlett Classick, who drove that Austin Healey 3000 up in the blistering time of 35.8, less than six seconds behind Penny Garnier and Eva Carlssen."

The long turquoise and cream sports car was shown being carefully driven into the paddock and reversed into a bay between the Porsche and the Jaguar. Wearing a striking pink polka-dotted crash helmet, the driver climbed out, to be greeted by an older woman.

"I believe that's Mrs Sarah Classick, Scarlett's mother and owner of that magnificent car.'

The return of the lady racers brought a swarm of onlookers into the paddock area, where each car was neatly garaged beneath a timber-framed lean-to shelter. While Formula 1's racing paddocks had long since become showy, high-tech mechanical laboratories, Shelsley's creosoted shelters retained their quaint rustic quality, akin to World War II air raid shelters.

"Right, just a few more minutes of preparation and I think we'll be getting a signal that the course is ready for the run-off. The race commentary has confirmed that Mrs Carlssen has opted to run first."

The screen now showed Eva slowly cruising her gleaming silver racer down to the start, drawing waves of encouragement from the crowd perched high above the start line. She acknowledged them like a veteran. As she pulled up to the line, a marshal in oily red overalls slipped a black rubber chock behind a rear wheel. She nonchalantly strapped on her silver crash helmet, pulled on her elbow-length snakeskin driving gloves and tightened the knot in the silk silver scarf she wore around her neck.

"Interesting, that Tom. Did you notice that Mrs Carlssen didn't bother to warm up her tyres on her approach to the start line? How cool is that?"

"I've always felt that tyre warming at Shelsley is 70% bravura and 30% racing efficiency. These days, in Formula 1, we see cars sat on the start line with their tyres wrapped in electric blankets. But for a short, up-hill dash of just one thousand yards, on a bone-dry track in conditions like we've got here today, tyre warming really won't greatly enhance your driving wheels' traction."

"Rather unusually, I see she's set the Spyder on the extreme left of the start line, close to the timing box. What's the reason for that, Andrew?"

"I can only think that she's opted to give herself a more pronounced angle of approach to the first left-hander, which is Crossing."

As the rear marshal removed the chock, the front marshal signalled three seconds remaining with his outstretched fingers. Eva stared intently at the hooded red and green start lights fixed to the marshals' cabin and gripped the steering wheel tightly.

"Three, two, one, she's off. Nice and clean and tidy."

Anthony felt a slight frisson of pleasure, as the Porsche's distinctive rasping crackle sounded across the kitchen. He willed the silver racer to make a smooth passage through Crossing.

"Wow. Now that was impressive! She barely lifted her foot, gently drifted it sideways and got into a perfect position for the challenging 'Bottom S' up ahead".

"I know you said earlier that these cars hug the road, but, my goodness, from up here it looks as if Mrs Carlssen was on rails as she went through 'Bottom S'!"

Anthony leapt from his chair with amazement, as the silver streak motored effortlessly through the last bend on the course – 'Top S' – before the final two hundred metre straight-line dash to the finish. Crossing the line, Eva raised both her hands from the steering wheel, akin to the exultant gesture beloved of Tour de France stage winners. Crowds waved enthusiastically all along the circuit at the gutsy performance.

"I've seen it on the timing screens out of the corner of my eye," said Sir Andrew Grimshaw, "but let's just wait for the official confirmation."

"30.02 seconds! Simply amazing! And from someone who had never driven up Shelsley Walsh before this morning! She's just shaved two hundredths of a second of her time. Well if that isn't throwing down the gauntlet, I don't know what is!"

The TV picture cut to a close-up of a grim-faced Penny Garnier, flanked by her mechanics. She stubbed out a cigarette, climbed into the cockpit of the D-type and fired up the 3–litre engine. It roared into life with a deep throaty growl.

As if to achieve maximum traction, the French driver spun her rear wheels as she left the paddock, making them snake violently, and then repeated the manoeuvre - producing even more tyre smoke - as she approached the start line. She opted for the centre of the track and, with a grimace, tugged her driving gloves on tightly and lowered her goggles.

Once again, the mighty Jaguar left its marks on the tarmac as the French woman sped away from the line. She conducted her car expertly through the shallow left-hand Kennel Bend, changed up a gear and set her line to go through Crossing. The dark green D-type was running perilously close to the right-hand grass embankment as she arrived at the left-hander's white-painted kerbing. A front offside wheel mounted the flat concrete surface.

"Oh dear. That's an unfortunate error. Unlike Formula 1, there's no advantage in clipping kerbs on hill climbs. I'm afraid that little error will probably have cost her one or even two hundredths of a second and... oh my GOSH!"

Though the commentary stopped abruptly, the dramatic TV pictures showed everything. The huge green Jaguar slewed sideways, then crashed through the metal safety fencing on the opposite side of the track. It reared up into the air - momentarily taking off - demolishing the scaffolding tower of a timing screen, before eventually landing in a dense pile of brambles, slowly rolling on its side like a beached whale. The driver remained motionless, strapped in her seat and slumped forward.

There was deathly silence amongst the crowd seated high up in the packed stands opposite. They waited for some sign of life from the driver's cockpit. The car's offside front wheel continued to revolve slowly, like a roulette wheel in a casino, before finally stopping.

Red flag-waving race marshals vaulted over the tangled metal fence, just as a medics' Land Rover came racing up from the paddock.

The two stunned television commentators tried to bring calmness to the visual mayhem. "That looks serious, but help is at hand. Let's go to the paddock, where we can see the next cars being lined up for their runs. We'll bring you news of Mademoiselle Garnier as soon as we have it."

Anthony remained frozen to the kitchen floor. Even Ben sensed the drama, jumping up and whimpering at his master.

Shots of sundry paddock activities followed, before the cameras finally permitted viewers to see a semi-conscious Pénélopie Garnier being placed on a stretcher which had been laid alongside her stricken car.

High up in the stands opposite, Anthony caught a fleeting glimpse of the Redknapps. While Walter sat studiously scrutinising his programme, Doris – wearing a brown cloche hat – was intently studying the accident scene through binoculars.

"Your thoughts, Andrew?"

"Well I have to say that accidents of the type we've just witnessed are extremely rare here at Shelsley. It's too early to speculate whether it was driver error or a mechanical malfunction, but just before we cut away from the crash scene, I did notice that there was only one black tyre mark on the track – probably made by the Jag's near-side front wheel – which would seem to indicate that only one of the car's disc brakes came on. Which, of course, could account for why poor Penny overcooked it going into 'Bottom S'."

Four marshals lifted the stretcher over the mangled fencing and placed it on the floor at the back of the Land Rover, which drove slowly down the hill in the direction of the paddock.

Anxious to add a final note of decorum, the TV commentator added: "Well that's all we have time for, I'm afraid. In a few moments we'll be returning to Lingfield, for the start of the William Gough Stakes. It looks as if it's going to take some time to extricate the poor old Jaguar from the brambles and to restore the safety barriers, before racing can continue.

"I see we've just had a message from Race Control to say that Mademoiselle Garnier is OK and in no danger, but as a precautionary measure the medics have decided that she should be flown to Hereford Hospital for checks. She'll be air-lifted out in that red helicopter you can just see touching down in the field behind the paddock. The note also says that the accident wasn't due to a driver error and that Penny's mechanics are reporting that the Jaguar's front nearside brake fluid pipe was sheared through, possibly from the car's impact with the edge of the steel fence.

"Right, that's all from us for this afternoon. Our special thanks to Sir Andrew Grimshaw, for his expertise and fascinating reminiscences. Now over to my colleague John McCririck at Lingfield."

Anthony picked up the remote and switched the TV off.

The sky darkened to the west, usually a sign of an incoming shower heading in from the Wrekin. He didn't need much of an excuse to postpone the gardening. Just before the first heavy splats of rain fell on the fish pool, he went outside and moved the plywood covers into place to prevent the trench from flooding.

He laid a log fire, fed the dog and decided to prepare a risotto supper for Barbara's return or for freezing if she was late. Then he browsed the Sunday papers by the fireside.

It was nearly 11.00p.m. when Anthony and Ben simultaneously heard the crunch of the Volvo's tyres rolling up the gravel drive. The little Sheltie bounded into the hall to welcome his mistress.

Anthony and Barbara embraced. 'Have you eaten?'

'Yes thanks. Steph and I had brunch before I set off.'

'I made one of my risottos, but it'll keep for tomorrow.'

She slipped off her driving coat. I'm afraid we had a rather late night after the premiere.'

'How was it?'

'The film or the party afterwards?'

'Both.'

'*Gambit 2* is OK. Fair-to-middling. It certainly won't get any Oscar nominations.'

'Poor Stephenie.'

'I don't think it was a very happy shoot.'

'And the party?'

'Brilliant! Lots of celebs. I felt quite out of it.'

'Why?'

'Well, she's a bit of a star, isn't she? British set decorators don't collect Oscars every day of the week.'

'What's her next movie?'

'It's not a movie, actually; it's a Harry Potter theme park; somewhere in China. I can't imagine why.'

'So what news of *"Hotel Majestic"*? Is there going to be a third series?

Barbara smiled for the first time. 'Looks like it. There's talk that filming may start before Christmas – and I've still got a job below stairs. With an added twist.'

'What's that, Barbara?'

'Well – it's only speculation at the moment – but they want to write a cameo part in for Johnny Depp.'

'Playing an aristo?'

'No! Playing a page boy. Who makes a pass at me!

'Lucky you.'

Barbara had been preparing herself a hot milk drink while she regaled her husband with the show business gossip.

'Would you mind awfully if I went to bed? I'm bushed.'

'Me too.'

'So what's worn you out?'

'Oh you know: walking Ben; tidying the house; gardening; cooking.'

His wife headed for the stairs with her mug. 'Hardly exhausting, I'd have thought', she said haughtily. 'Good night.'

Half-an-hour later Anthony followed Barbara upstairs. He climbed into bed without disturbing her.

Once again, his sleep was fitful and unsatisfying.

Eventually, with Barbara gently snoring beside him, Anthony went into a deep sleep, in which he had a lucid dream, revisiting his days as an English master at Birch Cross.

In the dream, he was seated in the staff Common Room, wearing his black gown and reading a book. Opposite him on a long sofa sat three fellow teachers – all in gowns and mortar boards – all reading the *Daily Telegraph*. A strange, semi-opaque mist of pale lavender hung in the air in sinuous horizontal layers.

The Common Room door was thrust open dramatically, to reveal Eva. She was wearing a pair of perilously-short, frayed-denim shorts over black fishnet, thigh-high stockings and diamante-studded platform high heels. Her diaphanous, off-the-shoulder red chiffon blouse was tied in a knot below her bust line, revealing a trim and sun-tanned midriff. Her chestnut curls were held in a top-knot by her signature tortoise shell hair grip. A thin purple aura enveloped her head and shoulders.

On her left forearm arm sat a small tawny owl, whose plumage she gently stroked, as a bird handler does with a hunting hawk. It had staring, emerald green eyes. A sports whistle hung on a silver lanyard from Eva's neck. The mist began to envelop her.

This, Anthony realised, was the new Games Mistress.

'Are you seriously intending to take hockey practice dressed like that?' he boomed across the room.

She smiled at Anthony and fluttered her long eyelashes, like Betty Boop. 'Haven't you ever seen a lady's navel before?'

In unison, the three schoolmasters looked up, startled, from their newspapers. Beneath their mortar boards were not human heads, but the puzzled faces of the three long-haired monkeys of the famous 'Hear No Evil, See No Evil, Speak No Evil' Japanese folklore trio.

Anthony awoke with a start. Down in the kitchen the dog was barking. He lay still, trying to discern what might have disturbed the little Sheltie. Perhaps a rabbit or a badger moving about in the corn field? He thought he could just make out the light crunch of the gravel in the driveway – a single, tentative footfall – then silence. He was soon asleep again.

# VII

## *The Emerald Ear Studs*

THE SIGHT of the unfinished Leylandii trench annoyed Anthony.

All along, he had planned to devote his Sunday to gardening. He hadn't expected to be distracted by the TV coverage of the hill climb, dramatic though it was.

The curious circumstances of the crash, which resulted in Eva's victory, still troubled him. Her claims of witchcraft were hard to accept, but a whole series of recent incidents had begun to give him cause for concern. There were never logical explanations. And far too many coincidences.

After their early-morning walk, he led Ben back into the kitchen and settled him in his basket. Then he took a mug of tea up to a sleepy Barbara.

As it was still only 8.15a.m., Anthony decided to cover up the open trench to minimise the risk of its 'detection' by any passing ramblers. As he was anchoring the plywood boards in place with bricks, Barbara appeared at the kitchen door in a summer housecoat.

'Anthony, have you got a minute before you go off to the shop?'

'Of course.' He walked back into the kitchen.

'What on earth were you doing out there at this hour?'

He removed his gardening gloves and boots. 'I was digging something up there yesterday – and got distracted; in the end I never got it finished.'

She ignored his mangled excuse, clearly having a more pressing matter to focus upon. Hands in her housecoat's pockets, she was staring down at two small jewelled objects on the kitchen table.

'Know anything about these?'

Set near the table edge were a pair of ear studs. They sparkled in the sunlight. Even his un-trained eye told Anthony that these were valuable items of jewellery: Victorian ear studs, with small round, brilliant-cut emeralds ringed by circles of tiny pearls. What was especially arresting about them was that they looked identical to the ear studs Eva had been wearing at the Codrington Manor fete.

'No. Where did you get them?'

'I found them just now in the downstairs loo. On the glass shelf over the wash basin. Alongside a vase with dead flowers in it.'

'Dried flowers?'

'DEAD flowers. VERY dead flowers! In a vase with no water.'

'How odd.'

'So what about the ear studs? Whose are they, Anthony?'

'I've really no idea. Perhaps they're Brenda's.'

'Brenda? I hardly think our cleaning lady would run to emerald and pearl ear studs like these! They aren't paste, you know. A Victorian pair like this would probably set you back about 4K at Melsons.' She turned one over curiously in her hand. 'What's more, they look remarkably like the ones that tarty woman was wearing at the fete last Sunday.'

'Really? I never noticed.'

'You didn't see what your friend was wearing on her ears? Frankly, I find that hard to believe. They stuck out like a pair of cycle lamps!'

She placed the stud carefully back by its companion on the table. 'So. Has she been here? While I've been away?'

'Who?'

'Who do you think? That tarty woman. Or Eva-the-diva, as Stephenie so aptly dubbed her.'

'No she certainly has not!'

'Are you sure, Anthony?'

'Certain.'

'Then how did her ear studs get parked in our downstairs loo, I'd like to know?'

'Search me.' He banged the kettle down on the Aga.

'When did you last see her?'

He shrugged nonchalantly. 'She called in briefly at the shop on the Monday after the fete.'

'What for?'

'She said she wanted to buy a new handbag.'

'I wasn't aware "Train Spotters" sold ladies' leather goods.'

'Barbara, don't be so pedantic. She came into Ludlow to buy a bag, and called in at the shop to say 'hello'. I told her to try "Just My Bag"'.

'Really?' The full theatrical Barbara came out, with a response of cynical disbelief. 'Somehow, I doubt they could have helped her. That shop sells quality goods. Your tarty lady friend would have been looking for something much more showy. Probably quilted white plastic with chrome chains and bells on, I dare say.' She scooped up the studs and put them in the pocket of her housecoat. 'And after that?'

'What do you mean?'

'When was the next time you two met up?'

'There hasn't been a "next time", Barbara.' Last Monday, when she called at "Train Spotters" was the last time I saw Eva.'

'And you haven't seen her since then?'

'No.' Anthony decided that television images could be excluded without perjuring himself.

Barbara tapped a small quantity of muesli into a bowl. 'Well my information is that she was seen driving through town in that... ridiculous silver Noddy car of hers, on Saturday.'

Anthony had no doubt who Barbara's informant was. 'Well I certainly didn't see her. We were too busy in the shop. I had Tim Nugent helping me.' He decided to cut and run.

'Now, if you've finished your... cross-examination, I'll just make myself a quick coffee and be off into town.'

Barbara added milk to her cereal, sat down at the table and ate her breakfast in silence. The dog observed the marital stand-off glumly.

Sloshing some un-boiled water from the kettle into a mug of instant coffee granules, Anthony felt he had acquitted himself adequately, without directly lying. But he was far from certain that the 'prosecuting counsel' was convinced. Though the court was now adjourned, a further cross-examination in the evening was inevitable.

He let himself out quietly, regained possession of his Volvo and set off to drive into town.

He managed to open the shop on time. The incoming mail was unexciting and he was relieved that none of the envelopes bore the town council's coat-of-arms. But there was an envelope from his solicitors which he knew would contain their account. Unduly prompt, he thought, given the lack of help he'd received. No wonder solicitors could indulge their wives with personalised number plates and showy 4 x 4s.

Tim Nugent rang in, full of enthusiasm about the following Saturday's visit by *Tornado*. He told Anthony he had spent the previous evening mugging up on the £3-million steam loco's provenance.

'I was thinking – this flyer you want me to hand out to the excursion passengers next Saturday at the station.'

'Yes. What's the problem?'

'No problem. It's just that I'm not due back at college until next week, so I've got some time on my hands at the moment. How would it be if I knocked up a rough layout and pinged it across to you later today? I think I could even download a picture of *Tornado* under steam from the trust's website. Their pics are copyright-free, you see.'

'Hey, that would be brilliant, Tim!'

'A5 you said, didn't you?'

'Yes, but we need to keep down the costs.'

'No problems. Just give me the e-mail address at the shop, will you, and I'll send you something to have a look at, at home this evening.'

Tim Nugent was better than his word and a very competent layout arrived in Anthony's computer in-box shortly before he slipped out to buy a sandwich for his lunch.

The shop's telephone was ringing when he let himself back into "Train Spotters".

It was a decidedly frosty Barbara. 'Anthony? Where on earth have you been?'

'I just nipped out to buy a sandwich and a cappuccino. Everything OK?'

'Everything is most certainly NOT OK!'

'What's the problem?

'The problem is that in your haste to leave the house this morning, you forgot to pick up your mobile phone. I found it on the kitchen worktop by the Aga.'

'No worries. I don't need it.'

'I think you do, Anthony. At just after 10.00a.m. it signalled that a text message had arrived. And as I thought it might be something to do with the shop, I opened it up.'

Anthony felt his body temperature fall rapidly. He didn't even need to ask the identity of the message's sender.

'Anthony? Are you still there?'

Yes, Barbara. I'm here.'

'The text message was obviously from that tarty woman, although it's simply signed "E", followed by a string of x's.'

'From Eva, you say?' How long could he play the dumb innocent, he wondered. 'What did she want?'

'She wanted you to go over to her cottage this afternoon to share a magnum of champagne with her. Said she was feeling lonely. And that's the expurgated version.'

He knew there were more excuses and explanations to be conjured up. 'Look, can we discuss this when I get home tonight?'

'By all means, Anthony. But I think I should tell you that, having opened up this latest text message, I felt I should just take a look at any others which you'd received while I was away. Especially as you assured me this morning that you hadn't seen this woman since the day after the fete.

'In all, there are seven messages. And most of them are either bawdy or downright filthy! That woman wants to wash her mouth out with Dettol!'

Anthony was stuttering now, praying for a customer to walk through the door. 'Err... you've got the wrong end of the stick, Barbara. I really think it would be better if we discussed this in a calm and rational way when I get home this evening. I'll try to be back soon after 6.00p.m. - provided we're not too busy here at the shop.'

'Very well. But it will be a cold supper.' ('More likely an extremely frosty supper' he thought.)

'Oh, and by the way: you'd better buy yourself a new mobile phone.'

'Why's that?'

'Because your old one's in the fish pond!'

As if to confound Anthony's belief that things couldn't get any worse, the next incoming call half-and-hour later - was from the diva herself.

'Such a pity you're not here, sweetie. We could have finished the champers together and then gone to bed. I always adored making love with you in the afternoon,' she rambled semi-coherently. 'Hey, didn't they make a film with that name once? Yes, they DID! With

Audrey Hepburn and that hunky fellow who made lots of cowboy films. When I smoked, I had a black cigarette holder just like Audrey Hepburn. Is she still alive?'

'I really couldn't say.'

After a suitable pause, Anthony described Barbara's discovery.

'Oooops! And did she see the one about what we got up to in that deserted cove in Corsica?'

'No, fortunately I'd deleted that one. But she's seen the one offering late-night phone sex'.

'Can't see what's to get upset about. Wallis Simpson and the Duke of Windsor were doing it 75 years ago.'

'Eva – your texts are the sort of garbage that teenagers send each other these days!'

'The trouble with your Barbara is that she's like that French dyke at Shelsley Walsh yesterday: they're both bad losers!' After a pause, she added: 'Garry Cooper - it was Garry Cooper in *Love in the Afternoon* wasn't it?'

Then the glug-glugging of a glass being refilled. 'You still there?'

'Yes, Eva. But are you?'

'Right as rain, darling!' Then another long pause. '*Bad Day at Black Rock*. Remember that one?'

To damp down his tension, he tried leafing through some till receipts with his spare hand. 'I beg your pardon?'

'I'm saying that that's another train movie you're missing. From the stop. Stock. Stock in your shop.'

'*Bad Day at Black Rock*?'

'Spencer Tracey and Dan Maskell'.

'Dan Maskell was a Wimbledon tennis commentator, Eva.'

'No he wasn't! Big fellow. In loads of war films. You know who I mean: sang "I was born under a wandering star"?'

'That was Lee Marvin.'

'That's what I just SAID! Spencer Tracey and Lee Marvin.'

'Eva: how much of that magnum have you had?'

'Barely half.'

'Straight?'

'Err no. As we're celebrating, I've been making Corsican champagne cocktails, with just the merest *soupçon* of brandy added. Remember how you used to mix them for me?'

'Eva, listen to me: this has got to stop!'

'Darling, you're too stressed. I've told you before, you need a break. You're obviously not getting on well with wifey. The Canaries would be JUST the thing. Get that nice young man who was in the shop on Saturday to cover for you. And spare a thought for me, for once. I won't be here forever you know.'

'Why, where are you planning to visit next after Shropshire?'

'I've always wanted to see Brazil: Rio, the Iguaçu Falls. Who knows, this time next year I might even be in Never-Never land. So let's have a little secret holiday together?'

'Eva, I'm sorry but the answer is the same at it's been every time you've suggested such an idea. Now I really must get some orders ready for posting tonight. I'll leave you to finish your champagne. Goodbye.'

The simmering row between Anthony and Barbara continued in the evening after he got home.

'It's totally beyond me why this woman suddenly turns up in Shropshire at all - if, as you claim, you haven't seen each other for six years.'

He shook his head with exasperation. 'Search me.'

'So - WERE you lovers?' Barbara crashed her knife and fork down on her plate for dramatic effect.

'In London? Err yes...' he adjusted his glasses and looked out of the kitchen window. '... yes, we did make love.'

'That was NOT what I asked, Anthony! Well, were you lovers?'

'Yes. But it didn't work out.'

'Why was that?'

'I found her too possessive. Too... demanding.'

Quietly placing his knife and fork together on the empty plate, he got up from the kitchen table. 'I think I'll just take a stroll in the garden. See if there's anything I need to remind the gardener about tomorrow.' Ben followed him outside.

Collecting a small fishing net from the back of the garage, Anthony approached the fish pond. He could clearly make out the screen of his phone nestling on the bottom amongst the weeds. After a couple of attempts, he managed to net it and bring it to the surface.

In the still evening air, he heard the flapping of a bird's wings. He looked up, to see a small tawny owl fly overhead. It swooped low over the corn field and then gently rose up, disappearing into the stand of tall elms which marked the edge of Barnard's Wood. The creamy edge of a harvest moon was just emerging above the trees.

# VIII

## *The Missing Weed Killer*

BARBARA HAD MOVED into the spare bedroom. Without taking any breakfast, Anthony decided to leave home early to avoid a reprise of the previous morning's cross-examination.

He opened up "Train Spotters" before 9.00a.m. The early morning gloom was sufficient for him to put the shop window lights on.

'Early riser?' Terry stood in the shop doorway.

'Didn't sleep too well. I expect I was worrying about that visit last week from the council's Disabled what's-it officer. Plus having to listen to Glenys Kinnock pontificating about illegal migrants on telly last night. That woman could talk for Europe.'

'Seems your life is plagued by difficult women.'

'Tell me about it!' Anthony sifted through the newly-arrived bills.

'Barbara back?'

'Yup. Got back Sunday night.'

'Everything OK?'

'Things have been better, shall we say.'

'What's the problem?'

'Oh, it's not Barbara – it's that bloody flame-haired temptress.'

'Little Eva? Hey - I saw her on the telly on Sunday afternoon. Blimey, didn't she throw that little Porsche of hers about!'

'I felt sorry for the French woman, though.'

Terry grimaced. Call me a male chauvinist pig, but - I'm sorry -

French women and classic British racing cars just don't go together, somehow. Why's Little Eva giving you grief?'

'She just won't leave me alone.'

'You should be so lucky! Give me her my phone number, mate. I won't kick her out of bed.'

'And what would Tina have to say?'

'Didn't you know? Tina and me hasn't been an item for nearly a year.'

'I'm sorry, I hadn't heard. But honestly, Terry, you couldn't handle her. She's a bloody menace. A sexual predator.'

'Lovely. Tell me more!'

'She's managed to get through three husbands…'

'Zsa Zsa Gabor's had nine!'

'… and I'm convinced she's stalking me. Know anything about stalking?'

'Not a lot. You read about it in the papers, of course. But I've never had no first-hand experience.'

'I need to talk to an expert.'

'Your local brief?'

'No thank you – not that shaven-headed pillock! His lot round the corner will charge you £50 for opening their office front door. When I went round to see him about this council threat of enforcement – remember, after you spotted that woman measuring my doorstep? What d'you think his professional advice was?'

'Go on, tell me.'

'"You haven't got a leg to stand on, old man." And the bill for £75 for that useless piece of information arrived in the post yesterday morning!'

'Local plod?'

'What do you mean?'

'Go and have a chat with your friendly local community officer. Say this woman's been pestering you.'

Anthony was unenthusiastic. He didn't relish the idea of walking into Ludlow police station. His mind raced back to the excruciating interview he had had with the Headmaster of his old school. A wholly one-sided interview, in which he was told: "The boy's parents wanted the local police to be brought in. But I advised against it, for the good of the school's reputation."

This had been his nearest brush with the police, and ever since then he had preferred to keep his distance from "the boys in blue". He shook his head. 'No, I'm really not keen. Terry.'

'Look, tell you what. I've got a mate in the Met down in London. He's pretty street-wise. Want me to talk to him?'

'Would you? I'd appreciate it if you would.'

'OK. So give me the low-down: what's Little Eva been up to, by way of stalking you? What's involved?'

When Anthony did a rapid mental run-through of the contact he had had with her over the previous nine days (they felt more like nine weeks), Eva's list of personal violations hardly seemed heinous.

'Well, to start with, she's turns up unexpectedly...'

'So did my in-laws.'

'... and she rings me at work and at home and sends me extremely salacious text messages...'

'That's hardly "stalking", mate. More like female flirtation, I'd say. Youngsters get up to it all the time. I'm told they even send each other selfie close-ups of their private parts!

'My understanding is that stalking's when a total stranger follows a young woman home who he's clocked, say, on the Underground, or coming out of the local supermarket, or whatever. Then he starts pestering her. That's stalking.'

'Well, the latest – if you can believe this - is that she wants to take me off on holiday to the Canary Islands.'

Terry folded his arms and smirked. 'And that's IT?'

'I know it all sounds pretty petty, but I can tell you, it isn't exactly creating domestic harmony in the Metcalf household, just at the moment. Barbara's on the point of walking out. Yesterday she found some of Eva's texts and flung my phone in the bloody fish pond! And, to be honest, I couldn't blame her.

'If you could have a word with your friend at Scotland Yard, I'd really appreciate it.'

'Leave it with me; I'll see what I can do. What I really came over for, was to ask if you'd rung Cyril the bookbinder?'

'Yes I have and the Bradshaw will be ready in three weeks.'

'Well done, my son. eBay here we come!'

The shop phone rang. Would it be Barbara or Eva, Anthony thought. Either of them would spoil his morning.

'I'd better go,' said Terry, excusing himself. In fact, the caller was the new gardener.

'Mr Metcalf? Mike Green. Sorry to trouble you at work. I've finished the trench, but I can't seem to find the weed killer. Did you get it?'

'Yes, I did, Mike. I put it on the top shelf at the back of the garage. Alongside all the lawn feeds, like we arranged.'

He heard the sound of heavy footsteps pacing down his garage floor. 'Top shelf?'

'Yes, Right next to a big box of bone meal.'

After a pause, the gardener came back on the line. 'The bone meal's here all right and a green one called "Ready Lawn". But I can't see no weed killer.'

'Big white tin with a blue nozzle?'

'No. There's only the bone meal and the lawn feed, with a gap between the two of 'em.'

'How odd. I could have sworn I put it up there. I'll have to get you another can. Ah well, we'll just have to postpone that little job for another week, I'm afraid.'

'Right you be, Mr Metcalf. In the mean time I'll just board the trench over again, shall I?'

'If you would, Mike. Maybe ask Mrs Metcalf if there are any other things around the garden she'd like you to attend to.'

'Will do.'

'Many thanks.'

As there were few customers, Anthony settled down to check Tim's flyer design for the shop's blitz on the forthcoming *Tornado* visit. It was a very workmanlike effort, which he slipped under the counter.

He collected up three packages he had to take to the Post Office. He would also call at Williams for a fresh can of weed killer and pick up his new mobile phone. But just as he had got his key in the front door lock, the phone rang.

'Good morning,' chirruped Eva. 'And how are we today?'

'Morning, Eva. I was just on my way over to the Post Office, actually.'

'Busy, busy. My man is always on the go. You know, Anthony, you really should slow the pace down a bit. You need a holiday. Somewhere warm. How's home life?'

'I'd rather not talk about it.'

'Oh dear. Wifey still miffed about the texts?'

'You could say that.'

'Well at least you've recovered your mobile phone.'

'My phone?'

'Yes, the one she threw in the fish pond.'

What makes you think I've got it back?'

'Anthony - not all witches have cats for familiars, you know. So what other excitements have you got planned for today, apart from experiencing the delights of Ludlow's Post Office? Not thinking of popping in to see Julia, I hope.'

He ignored the catty question. 'When I get back, I've got to try to get down to drafting an application for a short-term bank loan.'

'*Pour-quoi?*'

'Because I'm being leaned on by the council to get the entrance to this shop enlarged, so that wheelchair users can get in and out, would you believe?'

'More Blairite bollocks!'

'I couldn't have put it better myself.'

'Will it be expensive?'

'Probably. Six or seven K, I'd guess. Which, right at the moment, I don't have. A builder's due to come and give me a quote on Saturday.'

'Don't go grovelling to the bank, sweetheart. They're all blood-sucking crooks! Listen, why don't I lend you the money?'

Anthony was almost touched. Just when this woman could be utterly exasperating, or infuriatingly demanding, she would suddenly show compassion and generosity. But the last thing he wanted was to be indebted to her.

'Thanks for the offer, Eva. Let me think about it.'

'Of course.'

'I'm going have to dash. I want to post these packages before the noon deadline. Ring me this afternoon?'

'I will, honey bunch. Bye.'

After visiting the Post Office and the ironmongers, Anthony cut up Market Street, opposite Florian's, and had the misfortune to bump into Doris Redknapp leaving the butchers.

'Is your wife back yet, Mr Metcalf?'

'Yes, thank you Mrs Redknapp. She got back late on Sunday evening. The filming was a great success, I gather.'

'Oh how lovely. My Walter does like watching that series. When's it coming back?'

'October, I believe.'

'That's nice. I see that friend of yours was on the TV on Sunday. Did you watch it?'

'Err... the hill climb? Yes, I saw a bit of it.'

'Terrible about that accident, wasn't it?' Mrs Redknapp had now placed her shopping basket squarely on the pavement and was in full spate. Passers-by had to step into the gutter. Anthony saw no escape. 'And that poor French woman?'

'Yes, tragic.'

'They're saying it wasn't an accident, you know.'

Anthony wasn't quite certain who "they" were, but decided he had better humour the old trout. 'Really?'

'Oh yes'. She slipped down an octave, into a conspiratorial whisper. 'My Walter plays golf every week with the Regional Crime and Police Commissioner, you know. He was saying yesterday that one of the brake pipes on the front of that green racing car...'

'The D-type Jaguar?'

'That's the one. Well it seems one of its brake pipes had been cut through, would you believe? Doesn't bear thinking about, does it, Mr Metcalf?' He looked to see if he could spot her "aura", but all he could see behind her was the fluorescent glow of the blood-stained carcasses hanging in the butcher's shop window.

'No, indeed it doesn't, Mrs Redknapp. Still I hope she makes a speedy recovery – the French lady.'

She nodded, as if imparting more classified information. 'They flew her back to France this morning.' She picked up her basket from the pavement. 'Well I must get on. Do give Mrs Metcalf my best wishes, won't you?'

'I certainly will. Goodbye.'

But Barbara wasn't at home that evening for Anthony to relay Doris Redknapp's insincere salutation. Propped up on the salt cellar on the kitchen table was a curt message.

"Have gone over to Malvern to see Mother. She is still having problems with her new carer. Will ring later when I've sorted it out. Please get your own supper. B" At least the cross-examination was postponed.

Anthony walked around the garden tailed by the Sheltie. When only one of its owners was home, he would cling to them like a shadow, as if terrified of being abandoned.

The gardener's work was extremely tidy – another bonus for employing an ex-army man, Anthony decided. As he was putting the replacement tin of weed killer on the shelf at the back of the garage, he heard the house phone ring. It was Barbara calling from Malvern. Her tone was frosty.

'I've settled Mummy down for the night, but she's not at all happy.'

'What do you mean – unwell?'

'No, she's fit as a fiddle. For a ninety-year-old. No, it's this wretched Filipino carer they've foisted on her. The woman – I say "woman" advisedly; she looks about 12 – can barely speak English. And I'm pretty certain that she can't read the language at all!'

'Why does she need to be able to read English?'

'Because of the labelling on Mummy's medication! There are five separate sets of pills she has to take for her conditions. And they all have to be administered at set times and dosages, and in the correct order. I'm sure this new carer's not up to it. It really is most trying.'

'What's to be done?'

'Well obviously I'll be staying here tonight. Tomorrow I intend to go down to the council offices. I'm going to tell them I want this girl replaced, otherwise I'll be lodging an official complaint with the DHSS. I think I might ring the local MP, as well.' Anthony remembered that when it came to complaining, Barbara believed in over-kill.

'Is there anything I can do to help?'

'No thank you. I'm perfectly capable of sorting this one out myself. I'll ring you tomorrow at the shop after I've been down to the council offices.'

Just when he thought his wife's diatribe was at an end, Barbara concluded with an ultimatum.

'When I get back from Malvern, Anthony, I'll expect you to have resolved matters with that tarty woman one way or the other. It simply can't go on like this.'

# IX

## *Eva's Bombshell*

THE HOUSE PHONE was ringing when Anthony returned from his morning walk with the dog. He looked at the kitchen clock: 8.20a.m. Too early even for Barbara to have resolved her mother's medical problems, he thought.

It was an exited Eva. 'Darling – I just had to ring you and catch you before you went to work.'

'What is it, Eva?'

'I'm looking at some photos of this simply amazing hotel I've found on the internet. It's called the Hotel Santa Catalina.'

'Never heard of it. Where is it?'

'Las Palmas, in the Canary Islands. And listen to this – it was built in 1890. One hundred and twenty-five years old! You like old buildings, don't you?'

'Oh Eva, not that again! I've told you before, it's out of the question. Totally. Especially since Barbara's discovery of your text messages. She rang last night, and to say her tone was frosty would be a gross understatement.'

Eva softened her voice to a plaintive whisper. 'Just a week?'

'No way.'

'Five days then? Don't forget, it's my treat. It could be like a honeymoon!' Anthony's heart missed a beat. But Eva ploughed on with her fantasy ramblings. 'They've got a special offer on a penthouse suite at the moment. It's got its own sun roof and a private pool. Just imagine: sunbathing in the altogether and then skinny-dipping! Just like in Corsica, only twelve storeys up! *Magnifique, n'est-ce pas?*'

'Eva - you're wasting your time – and mine. Look I've got to go and open up the shop. Wednesday is market day. Good for trade.'

She gave an impish giggle. 'I do believe you're coming around to the idea, you stodgy old bookworm. By the way, when's wifey due back from Malvern?'

'Malvern? Who said anything about Malvern?'

'Anthony, sweetie, I love you dearly. But do you EVER listen to a word I say? I told you at that fete the other Sunday that I'm now a fully-fledged witch. Tracking the movements of hostile spirits is the easiest thing in the world. Talk later. Biyee!'

He sauntered slowly around the garden, stopping by the pool to study the calm water surface and to reflect on events. If only he could find such tranquillity.

He looked across to the closed garage door. He had already decided that Barbara's dramatic discovery of the ear studs and the simultaneous disappearance of the weed killer could hardly be put down to the work of a sneak thief. Eva's prescience over Barbara's phone calls and movements, could possibly be shrewd guesswork or perhaps even feminine intuition, though how she had discerned that he had recovered his phone from the fish pond continued to baffle him. He lifted the garage door to take the Volvo out and drive into Ludlow.

The stalls in the central square were already decked out with their blue-and-white canvas awnings, and stocks were being unloaded from vans. Terry and Tina were unpacking cardboard boxes of bric-a-brac. Anthony stopped beside the couple. 'Weather forecast says it's set fine for the next three days.'

Terry nodded his head towards the unopened fish-and-chip shack which marked the back of the trading zone. 'Got a moment?' The two men ambled across, leaving Tina unpacking and setting out small items of Victorian china.

'I had a word with that mate of mine in the Met last night. He says stalking's still a very grey area.'

'Meaning what?'

'Meaning that it's too new an anti-social phenomenon – that's what he called it – for there to be many hard-and-fast rules. Apparently, it's all down to what's called "case law" – where the Crown Prosecution Service has successfully prosecuted. That lays down the markers, so to speak, over what constitutes out-and-out stalking. He says you should take a look at the CPS website for guidance. And the other thing he said the local police will want to know – that's if you go to report her – is: "has your personal freedom been infringed"?'

'My what?'

'I know – it's all psycho-babble; that's all coppers talk nowadays. "'ello, 'ello, 'ello" is long gone!'

'Well, I suppose if you class being sent lewd unsolicited text messages an infringement, then yes, my personal freedom has been infringed. My wife certainly thinks so!'

Terry looked across at his white van, where Tina was trying to man-handle a mahogany cabinet from the back.

'I'd better go and give her a hand. Why don't we meet up for a beer tomorrow evening after work? Talk it over? And we need to plan our eBay strategy.'

'Good idea. Where do you fancy?'

'The Old Bull Ring Tavern?'

Anthony grimaced. 'I'd rather not. Thursday is their karaoke night. It can get a bit raucous in there. How about the Feathers?'

'Fine. I'll see you in the Feathers at 6.00p.m. tomorrow.'

After opening up his bookshop on the Thursday morning, Anthony put in a call to Tim Nugent to compliment him on his flyer design.

'Well if REME won't have you, I think you'd make an excellent graphic designer.'

'Really? Did you like it?'

'I liked it so much I'm going to go out later and get an A3 blow-up to stick in the shop window. Listen, do you feel like helping out again this Saturday?'

'Sure.'

'Shall we make it all day this time?'

'Fine. I can be in by 9.00a.m.'

'OK, see you on Saturday.'

Barbara confined her communications to texting Anthony on his new mobile phone, which now never left his pocket. Her latest text told him that she had managed to get an appointment to see the head of the town's primary health care trust later that day. In consequence, she would be staying another night with her mother, but planned to return home on the Friday evening.

Anthony was relieved, not only because the "pressure cooker atmosphere" in the house would be absent for another 24 hours, but because it would enable him to relax and have a few ales with Terry in The Feathers Hotel after work.

Though he had managed to rescue the SIM card from his old phone, Anthony realised that this wouldn't deter Eva from sending saucy messages or ringing him. Her latest duly arrived just after 3.00p.m. It was a bombshell.

'Guess where I've been?'

'I give up.'

'Leominster.'

'Why?'

'I've been to the travel agents to collect our tickets.'

'"Our" tickets? What tickets?'

'Our flight tickets for the Canaries, silly! And guess what: the penthouse we've been allocated is the hotel's Honeymoon Suite. How about that for a coincidence?'

'Eva, I've told you this until I'm blue in the face: it's out of the question. I can't possibly get away.'

She lapsed into a soft, plaintive mode. 'But I did like you suggested and just made it five days – Saturday through to Wednesday. You can easily get that nice boy to cover for you at the shop. We're flying from Birmingham, by the way.'

'Eva, can I ring you back? I've got a customer.'

'Of course you can.'

There was no customer. Anthony just needed to calm himself down and think through a once-and-for-all rejection of this besotted woman's crazy plan. Do it with reasoned calmness? Or adopt the role of Mr Shouty Man?

But any decision was delayed by a gaggle of noisy tourists, who took a good half-hour to thoroughly inspect his stock, disturb his bookshelves and DVDs and then leave without making a single purchase. To add insult to injury, they asked directions to Ludlow Castle.

'Sorry about that, Eva, we've been really busy this afternoon. Look, that really was a bit of a curve ball you pitched me earlier, wasn't it?'

'How so, sweetie? I thought it was all arranged.'

'No it was NOT all arranged! NOTHING has been arranged. Nothing, *nada*, *rien*. Barbara is still on the fucking warpath! She's hopping mad - though mercifully she's now engaged in hostilities with the Chief Executive of Malvern PCT, poor sod. But I'll be back in the firing line tomorrow morning, for sure.'

There was silence on the line. Eva, Anthony guessed, had gone into sulky mode. 'Are you still there, Eva?'

'Yes. But I'm most terribly hurt, Anthony. And bitterly disappointed.' Now would come the Bridget Bardot pout. 'I think I'm going to go for a long walk.' The line went dead. He imagined himself walking beside her, her head rested affectionately against his arm.

Ludlow's 17th century Feathers Hotel in Corve Street is generally rated as the town's social centre, whether as an informal place for teenagers to hang out, or for be-suited Rotarians to foregather.

Due to its strategic significance in the 15th and 16th centuries, when Ludlow was the headquarters of the Council of The Marches, the Shropshire market town became the hub of regional government. For over two hundred years, the Council was the administrative base for the marcher lordships created by the English sovereign, which extended westwards into Wales. Because of all the activity generated, the town once boasted four coaching inns. The ornately-half-timbered Feathers Hotel is the sole survivor in its original form.

Terry had already taken up a quiet corner bench in the oak-beamed Lounge Bar, and had got their first round of drinks in when Anthony arrived.

'How's your day been?' the Cockney trader asked.

'I've known better. You?'

Terry pulled a face. 'Not too brilliant. The bleedin' tourists handle the goods, but don't buy nothing. Then they swan off to go to look at the castle.'

'Same here.'

'So what's Little Eva been up to?'

Anthony took a long pull on his lager. 'You're never going to believe this.'

'Try me.'

'What's the most outlandish stunt she could pull, do you suppose?'

Terry finished his lager and wiped his mouth with the back of his hand. 'She's going to give you the Spyder.'

'Almost as crazy.'

'Go on, tell me.'

'She's only gone and booked us a holiday in the bloody Canary Islands – staying in the honeymoon suite of a 5-star hotel in Las Palmas! What a crackpot idea.'

'Struth!'

'I was moved to use stronger language than that when she told me this afternoon. Same again?'

'Cheers, mate.'

On his return with the drinks, Anthony observed *soto voce*: 'I see the rolled-up trouser brigade are in tonight.' He nodded across at a table of eight middle-aged men, all in dark suits, sitting in the far corner of the bar.

'Must be their monthly Masonic meeting. Divvy-ing out all the best jobs in Ludlow, I expect,' said his friend sarcastically. 'So where's the missus this evening?'

'Malvern, visiting her mum.'

'Oh yes? Wouldn't have anything to do with your racing driver girlfriend with the nice gams, would it?'

'Ex-girlfriend, if you don't mind. Let's just say there was a minor domestic incident yesterday and Barbara got the hump.'

Terry took a reflective sip from his lager. 'Still got the hots for Little Eva, have you?'

'Don't be daft! The woman's a bloody menace - and a stalker to boot. The sooner I can get shot of her the better.'

'Did you take a look at that CPS website?'

'I haven't had time. I'll try to do it this evening.'

'How long is the Shropshire stalker staying?'

'That's what I'm not sure about. When I bumped into her at that Codrington Manor fete, I'm pretty sure she told me she'd rented the cottage at Bishop's Frome for a fortnight. She obviously needed it as a base because she'd entered the hill climb. With any luck she'll be gone by the weekend.'

Anthony sipped his beer ruefully then added: 'Though from past experience, that woman changes her mind as often as the wind. So she could still be here at Christmas!'

'Is she well off?'

'Loaded.'

'Really?'

'Divorced her first husband – an Italian surgeon living in Florence

– when she discovered he was keeping a mistress. Then she moved to Deauville and hooked up with a wealthy hotel and casino owner, who died of a heart attack. Then about three years ago, she married a Swedish industrialist and moved to Oslo. He popped his clogs earlier this year.'

'Now she's a sort of globe-trotting merry widow?'

Anthony pursed his lips, considering the comparison. 'Mmmm. No, I'd say she's not really like the Franz Lehár character – except that they're both filthy rich. Eva's more a Violetta. Or a Mimi or even a Tosca, if you know your Puccini. She's volatile but vulnerable, quixotic and terribly insecure.'

He recalled Eva's tearful reaction to the final scene in the Puccini opera *Madame Butterfly*, which they had once witnessed together in London.

'To tell you the truth, if Eva was to emulate Cio-Cio-san, that would solve all my problems.' The operatic analogy was lost on Terry.

'And now she's on the loose again?'

'Yup.'

'And looking for husband number 4?'

Anthony glumly sipped his lager. 'Seems so. And yours truly is the principal target, even though I'm happily married. Or was until Monday morning.'

'Time for another half?' Terry asked his companion.

'OK, then I'm going to shoot off. I want to take the dog for a good long walk before it gets dark.'

Terry returned with their drinks. 'So when's the missus due back?'

Anthony smiled. 'She's keeping her cards close to her chest with that one. I think she's hoping to catch us *in flagrante delicto*.'

'Is that likely?'

Anthony glanced across the lounge bar. 'I'd say there's about as much chance as me being elected next Grand Master of the Lodge of The Marches!'

Terry chuckled, as the line of dark-suited Masons trooped upstairs in single file to a meeting room, carrying their slim black leather cases. In an effort to draw Anthony out of his morbid reverie, he asked: 'About the Bradshaw; what's our next move?'

Anthony blinked away his malign thoughts. 'Yes, sorry. Well, I've got a young man helping me out at the shop at the moment. He's coming in again on Saturday and he's a wizard with computer graphics. I thought I might ask him to work out an eBay text for us with an image, if you're agreeable.'

'Sure.'

'I'll pop over to Cyril's at the weekend and get a picture of the Bradshaw on my phone.'

'And how will we go on for paying this lad?'

'Tim Nugent? Well, if we get him to put it up on eBay for us - at, say, £300 – we could offer him a nice little 5% commission on whatever it fetches. Let him handle all the bidding. What do you think?'

'Good idea.'

'OK, I'll talk to him about it on Saturday.'

'So what have you got planned for tonight?'

'Not a lot. Welsh rarebit watching *Question Time*, I expect.'

'Well as George Galloway's on the panel, I should think you'll be having an early night, mate!

Un-characteristically, Anthony meandered home. It wasn't from any reluctance to actually be home; or to see his little Sheltie; or even to know that there would be no incoming "hostile fire" from Barbara this evening. It was the invisible sinister aura which he felt was now following him; enveloping him.

He pulled into a leaf-strewn lay-by at the top of the short wooded descent, a mile from Kynaston. The last of the day's sunshine was spread, like a huge orange carpet, across the shallow, trough-shaped valley which the barn overlooked.

Barnard's Wood was positively iridescent. A small tawny owl flew out of the wood, encircled the Metcalfs' house and then flew off towards the south-east. Like a carrier pigeon.

Ben barked furiously on hearing his master's car arrive. Anthony pampered him, fed him and calmed him down. The stroking of the dog's lush mane eased his own stress.

'So what's it to be, old friend?' he enquired after the dog had bolted down his supper. 'A vigorous hike up to Barnard's Wood, or an early night in front of the telly?'

The little Sheltie didn't need much persuasion and happily curled up at his master's feet in front of the fire. There was a succession of news broadcasts, followed by the BBC's weekly political knock-about.

The four pugilists in the ring were the former Respect leader, the Scottish Nationalist's feisty Nicola Sturgeon, the glamorous *Antiques Road Show* presenter Fiona Bruce, and Labour stalwart Diane Abbot. It looked as if Galloway was in for a feminist mauling, and the presenter quickly ducked behind the ropes.

After two acrimonious rounds of so-called debate, Anthony had had enough. Ben settled in his basket, while his master slowly roamed the garden. Long shafts of milky-yellow moonlight washed across the cornfield. The warm night air was intoxicating.

As he stood on the temporary boards which covered the dreaded trench, which was soon to bring death to the tall green hedge, he looked across to Barnard's Wood. He recalled the noise of the little owl's wings, as it flew low over his head the evening when he had recovered his phone from the pool. No owls tonight.

With the discordant bickering of the politicians still ringing in his ears, Anthony trudged upstairs to bed. He paused on the landing to glance out of the small window which gave a view of the lane leading down to the house.

The trees along the verge had cast a dark serpentine line along the road. On the opposite side, in the shadows, he could just make out a small figure, wearing a long black coat. A poacher? Maybe a curious youngster from the neighbouring farm. It was standing perfectly still and looking directly – and intently - towards him. For several moments, they attempted to out-stare each other. Neither flinched.

Then the mysterious 'watcher' turned and walked away.

# X

## *An Inspector Calls*

THE ANTIQUE Citröen 2CV of Jenny Preece putt-putted its way cautiously up Honeysuckle Cottage's gravel drive, stopping behind the tenant's silver Porsche Spyder. The sports car's red tonneau cover was fastened across the cockpit.

'Oh lawks. That's always a bad sign,' said the driver to her passenger as she peered through the windscreen.

'What's up, Mum?'

'Why, when they're still in residence. It's hand-over day, girl, and we've only got jist over two hours to get the place ready for when that party from West Bromwich arrives, you know.'

'It'll be OK.'

'I ain't so sure. In my experience, one woman on her own can make a terrible lot of mess.'

The older woman eased herself off the little Citröen's canvas seat, pulled down her skirt, and approached the steps leading up to the tiled porch. She looked back at her car and called out: 'The other thing in this business is, Sod's Law says: "When the last lot leaves late, the next lot always arrives early!" She chuckled to herself at the joke.

Although she held the entrance key in her hand, Jenny Preece felt it prudent to knock loudly on the front door. She knocked a second time, looked back at her daughter and pulled a face.

'What d'you reckon, Kath?'

'What do you mean, Mum?'

'Well if 'er car's 'ere in the drive, why ain't she answering?'

'Still in bed? Maybe she's gone for a walk?'

'Lawks-a-Mussy, Kath! Fine time to take a walk, in't it?'

The old woman slotted the iron key into the lock and let herself in.

'Mrs Carlssen?' Her call echoed up the stairwell beside the cottage's tiny entrance hall. 'Mrs Carlssen? Cleaners!'

Getting no response from the tenant she was relieving, the elderly cleaning lady called back to her daughter: 'Reckon you're right, girl. She must be out walking. Come on: we'll make a start afore she gets back!'

Strewn across the entrance hall's oak-boarded floor, like wedding confetti, were pages ripped from a Yellow Pages trade directory. A coat rack, along with several scarves and woollen hats, had been dumped on top of the paper litter. A gaping hole in the plastered wall revealed where it had been ripped out.

Jenny Preece nervously peered through the opened kitchen door, while her daughter hovered on the threshold.

'Mrs Carlssen? Alright to come in and start tidying up, is it?' A bedroom door upstairs banged in the draft.

The housekeeper looked at her watch, which showed 10.15a.m. She knew from experience that the enthusiastic West Midlanders would be drawing up outside in ninety minutes. 'Come on, girl. We'd better crack on. You do downstairs, while I goes up and tackles the bedroom.'

'Right you be,' said her reluctant daughter.

Kath walked into the small kitchen, which was barely four times the size of the entrance hall. The small square table in the centre of the quarry-tiled floor was empty, save for a single mug. The worktops flanking the sink were bereft of china or any evidence of cooking, and the only item in the sink was a dirty plate stained with dried tomato sauce. As she moved to the sink, Kath kicked a bottle which was lying on the floor.

'Much to do down there, Kath?' came a call from the upstairs bedroom.'

'Seems she's not 'ad no breakfast', the housekeeper's daughter called, picking up the empty brandy bottle from the kitchen floor and dropping it in the rubbish bin.

Jenny Preece leant over the landing rail and bellowed: 'There's black rubbish bags under the sink. Clear out the fridge and pantry, empty all the litter bins and take the bags outside. I'll take 'em down to the dustbin afore we goes. We ain't got time for polishing. Then you'd better come up 'ere and give me a hand. This bedroom looks like it's been 'it by an 'urricane!'

The cottage's principal bedroom, decorated in a pastel Laura Ashley wallpaper, looked as if it had been vandalised.

The mattress was skewed across the double bed and its sheets and pillows lay in the furthest corners of the room. Pictures and a mirror hung at crazy angles on the wall and a large pile of glass debris – once perfume bottles and make-up jars – lay beside the dressing table. The overall impression was that a violent struggle had taken place.

A dazed Jenny Preece walked over to the bedroom window. She gazed at the footpath which ran alongside the wood behind Honeysuckle Cottage, in the forlorn hope that she might catch sight of Eva Carlssen returning from her walk. Her daughter stood in the doorway surveying the carnage.

'S'truth, Mum – what's been goin' on?'

'Search me, darlin'. Done the kitchen?'

'As far as I can.'

'Right, let's get this mattress back on the bed, shall we? Then you go and fetch the clean bedding from the car. We'll make the last job bath towels, tea towels and the flowers. Then I reckon the West Brom lot will be 'ere, so we can push off.'

Surprisingly, the tiny bathroom which adjoined the cottage's principal bedroom was spotless. Even its towels hung in straight lines from the towel rails and the face cloth draped over the wash basin was bone dry.

The two women swept up the glass fragments and emptied the bedroom waste basket into a black rubbish bag and returned to the ground floor. It was just after 11.00a.m.

'Hey, we've done real well girl. Just stick them two pints of milk from the car in the fridge will you, while I nip down and dump the rubbish?'

'What about her car parked outside?'

Jenny Preece picked up the two bulging rubbish bags and slung one over each of her ample shoulders. 'Nothin' to do with us, darlin'. That's down to the tenant.'

After wiping down its shelves, Kath placed the two milk cartons in the fridge and then gave the laminated worktops a cursory polish.

Her mother trudged down the narrow cottage garden, towards a small weather-boarded shed, alongside which was a single galvanised dustbin. Jenny Preece always made this her final job.

Today, the appearance of the lop-sided shed and its neighbouring dustbin looked somehow different. As she drew closer, she saw that the tenant had already deposited a large quantity of rubbish up against the side of the shed. It appeared to be several pillows, covered over by a rug. And sticking out from beneath this pile of rags was a tartan kilt. There was also an empty champagne bottle.

She tut-tutted to herself, imagining another half-hour's labour for herself and Cath to bag up all the old rags, when all they wanted to do was get away before the next tenants arrived.

She dropped the black plastic bags on the ground, advanced towards the heap and gave it a sharp kick, causing it to lurch sideways away from the shed. In the space revealed between the base of the debris and the corner of the garden shed was a stockinged leg. Contorted alongside the leg was a stark white arm, with a clenched fist.

Jenny Preece dropped to her knees and retched violently, spewing vomit onto the grass. Then she began sobbing.

It was the call of her daughter several minutes later that brought her back to reality. 'Come on Mum!'

She got up slowly and staggered back to the cottage. Kath was standing on the top step. 'What's up, you look awful,' the girl said. Her mother slumped down onto a step, bending her head low until it was almost in her lap.

The younger woman descended the steps and placed a hand gently on her mother's shoulder. 'Mum? What's the matter?'

Jenny shook her head slowly. 'Don't go down to that shed, girl; just DON'T go!'

Within the hour, Honeysuckle Cottage had been cordoned off by striped 'SCENE OF CRIME' tapes. Three police cars and two police vans were parked irregularly along the lane. Uniformed and overalled police officers, forensic specialists and photographers moved in and out of the cottage, watched by a small knot of local residents. The bemused West Bromwich family sat forlornly in their family saloon.

An unmarked black police car pulled up and a tall thin man, followed by a young uniformed West Indian woman police officer approached the cottage. Jenny Preece and her daughter were standing near the front door. The man walked up to them.

'Would you be Mrs Jenny Preece?' Jenny nodded. 'Good morning, madam. Detective Inspector Benjamin. This is my colleague Detective Sergeant Tierney.' He adjusted his rimless glasses and looked at Kath. 'And would this be your daughter?' Jenny nodded. 'Which of you two ladies found the body?'

Seeing her mother was close to tears again, Kath spoke for the first time. 'Mum did.' The detective sergeant began taking notes.

'Whereabouts?' Jenny nodded her head at the garden shed, around which three white overalled policemen were probing the ground with metal rods.

'Over there. It was up against the side of the shed.' The inspector strolled across the lawn, but didn't speak to the trio of workers. He noted the set of white pegs in the grass, before returning to the three women.

'Mrs Preece: I'm sorry to cause you distress, especially having to have this chat out here. But I suspect it's a lot noisier in there right now. Can you tell me what state the victim's bedroom was in when you first arrived?'

'Dreadful. I've never seen such a mess. Clothes and furniture thrown everywhere. Broken glass. Even a picture ripped off the wall.'

'So it would be fair to say, would it, that some sort of violent struggle had gone on?' Jenny pursed her lips and nodded.

Dave Benjamin gestured to the woman detective to follow him back to their car. 'Excuse us for a moment, Mrs Preece?'

The two detectives stood by the car, with their backs to the cottage. 'Forensics will have collected whatever they can from the bedroom, but of course everything's going to have the cleaning ladies' prints on it too. You'd better arrange to get them to come into the station at Ludlow to give us sets this afternoon, and you can take statements at the same time. They'll be calmer by then. Send a car.' The woman detective nodded and returned to speak to the two cleaners.

A uniformed policeman wearing blue plastic gloves emerged from the cottage and handed Detective Inspector Benjamin a snakeskin wallet without speaking. Benjamin opened it to reveal two maroon passports, side-by-side. One bore the familiar coat of arms of the United Kingdom, while facing it was a travel document, labelled "SVERIGE PASS" above the distinctive triple crowns of Sweden. He slipped the wallet into his inside pocket just as his mobile phone rang.

'Benjamin.'

'Dave – it's Ted Hancock.'

'Morning Ted.'

'Nasty business.'

'Yes and the trouble is, much of the evidence was cleaned or polished away before we got here. What have the pathology people got to say?'

'That's really why I'm ringing. They say they can ping a cause of death report across to your phone by 6.00p.m. But it'll only be their preliminary findings.'

'Fair enough. And the likely time of death?'

'They're saying that's going to be a bit more problematical.'

'Why's that?'

'Well, we had a heavy frost last night, if you remember. Seems it plays havoc with the effects of rigor mortis. They say they've got other ways of arriving at a precise time, but it'll take them a bit longer.'

'Fair enough. Listen, young Rachel's bringing the two cleaning ladies in later. Alert finger prints, would you? And lay on an interview room.'

'Will do.'

'Now I've just got one more little problem you may be able to help me with, Ted.'

'Fire away.'

'I've got a carload of extremely disappointed folk here from West Bromwich, who were hoping to start their holiday in the cottage today. Obviously there's no way we're going to be finished with it for a couple of days. Any ideas what we can do with them?'

'Leave it with me, Dave. I'll get back to you shortly.'

The inspector put his phone away and walked across to join his colleague. He pulled the passports wallet out and handed it to her. She nodded. 'Dual nationality, eh?'

'Did either of you ladies meet the tenant, Mrs Carlssen?'

Kath and her mother shook their heads. 'Hand-overs often take place with us leaving the key under the doormat,' said the older woman, now more composed. 'And unless there's any problems

– which there weren't with this lady – we only see them at the very end.' The awful significance of this statement only occurred to Jenny Preece after she had delivered it, causing her to start crying again.

Two hours later the West Bromwich family were on their way down the lane leading away from Honeysuckle Cottage, to spend the night in a Travel Lodge on the A49 outside Ludlow.

Anthony and Ben sat in front of a cosy log fire at the far end of the old barn. A huge brick-clad chimney stack rose up to the timber-framed roof. The stone end walls flanking it were pierced by narrow lancet windows, hung with tapestry curtains, each surmounted by swags of dried hop vines.

The outside air temperature had dropped while Anthony was walking the Sheltie and he had decided to have a welcoming log fire to greet Barbara on her return from Malvern. Their cleaning lady had been during the day, leaving the vast terra cotta tiled floor glistening and smelling of bee's wax. On the oak refectory table in the centre of the old barn's long double-height space, was a Chinese bowl, filled with cut roses interspersed with lavender stalks. Though Anthony had taken the lavender from the garden, he had wisely bought the roses in Ludlow.

Henry Purcell's baroque operetta *Dido & Aeneas* was playing on the CD player and the haunting sounds and voices soon had Anthony gently nodding off. Dido's plaintive final lament wafted through the barn.

> *When I am laid, am laid in earth, may my wrongs create,*
> *No trouble, no trouble, in thy breast.*
> *Remember me... remember me...but ah forget my fate.*

He awoke to silence. The music had finished and the fire had burned down to a series of glowing red embers. The little Sheltie at his feet perked up on hearing a car roll slowly up the gravelled drive.

Half-awake, Anthony gazed upwards, to where the two angles of the barn's roof joined, beneath a decorated ridge plate.

Reflecting on the roof panels was a throbbing blue light.

The door knocker was rapped firmly twice. Anthony got up and, barely awake, shuffled towards the hallway. He swung open the big oak front door.

'Mr Metcalf? West Mercia Police.'

The tall stooping figure of Detective Inspector Dave Benjamin stood in front, holding out an identification card, with the petite Detective Sergeant Rachel Tierney standing behind him, carrying a large black filing box. 'May we come in?'

Anthony didn't want to appear inhospitable, but he needed to know why these two police officers were calling on him at nine o'clock at night.

'Is there a problem?'

'Perhaps I could explain the nature of this call... if we could step inside, Mr Metcalf?' The upward inflection at the end of the statement, while not sounding threatening, left the householder in little doubt that the two police officers waiting on the threshold, wouldn't be taking "no" for an answer.

'Very well, you'd better come in.'

'Thank you, sir.'

Anthony led the way while Ben brought up the rear.

As they emerged into the barn's lofty hall space, the two officers looked slowly around at the interior. Without invitation, Benjamin moved towards the long refectory table and nodded to the young policewoman to take up a position on the left-hand side, while he moved to the right, placing a hand on the back of a dining chair.

'All right if we sit here, sir?'

Anthony moved to the far end of the table, after sliding the flower vase to the side so that their vision wouldn't be obscured. He gripped the edge of the table. 'Of course.' Ben moved away, to curl up in front of the fire.

The three sat in silence around the table. Rachel Tierney took out a small black notebook and unclipped a pen from her tunic pocket. Dave Benjamin removed his mobile phone and placed it on the table in front of him.

'What can I do for you, Inspector?'

'We are making enquiries concerning the death earlier today of Mrs Eva Carlssen.'

Anthony drew his breath in slowly and then exhaled. He fixed his gaze on the pattern on the Chinese porcelain flower vase. He knew that both sets of eyes were focussed on his first reactions. He removed his hands from the table and placed them lightly on his knees. He could feel them trembling.

He slowly moved his vision up to engage with Benjamin's steely stare. 'When and where did this happen?'

'Mrs Carlssen's body was found this morning in the garden of the holiday cottage she had been renting at Bishop's Frome. Time of death, as yet unknown.'

'I see. And the cause of death?'

'We're awaiting a toxicology report, sir. But the circumstances are suspicious. May we have your full name?'

'Anthony Ellington Metcalf.' Rachel Tierney scribbled away.

'Unusual middle name.'

'My father liked jazz.'

'And you live here with your wife, I believe?'

'That's right.'

'Is she home, sir?'

'No, she's on her way back from Malvern. She's been visiting her elderly mother there.' Benjamin nodded.

'I understand that you are the proprietor of a book shop in Ludlow.'

'That's correct, inspector. "Train Spotters". It's in the market square.'

'I know it, sir.'

The senior detective paused, as if removing a pair of imaginary gloves. With the courteous 'preliminaries' out of the way, he could now concentrate on the real questioning. His eyebrows were raised slightly as he asked: 'I believe you knew Mrs Carlssen?'

'Yes inspector.'

'And how would you... describe the nature of your relationship with the lady?'

Anthony tried to make the answer as insignificant and casual as possible and gave a slight shrug. 'We were old friends.'

'Known her long, had you?'

Anthony nodded and looked up at the barn roof, genuinely searching for distant dates. 'I believe we first met around 2008. In London.'

'And had you kept in touch over the years?'

'No, not at all. Until about a week ago I hadn't seen or heard from Mrs Carlssen for years.'

'I see. Then your paths crossed again.'

'In a manner of speaking, yes.'

'Where was this, sir?'

'Codrington Manor. At a fete there, the Sunday before last.' Benjamin glanced across to check that the young woman had noted the date.

'And after that?'

'How do you mean, inspector?'

'After this encounter at the fete, did you see Mrs Carlssen again?'

'Once.' The reply seemed to disappoint the policeman.

'Just the once?'

'Yes.'

'Where was this, sir?'

'Mrs Carlssen called at my book shop on the day following the fete and we went and had a coffee together in Florian's. Just social chit-chat, you understand, for half-an-hour or so. Then she left to go off, to buy a handbag, I think it was.'

'And that was the last time that you saw Mrs Carlssen?'

'In the flesh, yes.' Anthony regretted the phrase as soon as he had uttered it.

'I'm sorry, sir?'

Rachel Tierney stopped writing and looked up.

'"In person", I should have said. I'm sorry. I briefly saw some images of her on television last Sunday. She was competing at Shelsley Walsh. In the hill climb.'

'Yes, we found the Paddock Car Park sticker on the windscreen of the lady's car.'

Anthony desperately wanted a drink of water to soothe his throat. He was damned if he was going to offer the two visitors coffee or tea.

He rose from the table and walked across to the kitchen. 'I'm just going to get myself a glass of water. I'll be right back.' He returned with a tumbler and settled down to resume the interrogation.

Dave Benjamin looked across at his detective sergeant. 'If we could just return to your earlier friendship with Mrs Carlssen, sir? I think you said it was six years ago.'

'About that, inspector. I can't be too precise without looking it up in some old diaries.'

'Quite so. And how would you describe that... earlier relationship?'

'How?'

'Yes, sir. Were you and Mrs Carlssen at that time... lovers?'

'Yes, we were, inspector. We were both single. Of course she wasn't Mrs Carlssen then.'

'So what was her name at that time?'

'Perrier.'

'Same spelling as the French fizzy water?' asked the woman detective.

'Same spelling; same dynasty.'

'And how long did the relationship last?'

'Four months. Sixteen weeks.'

'You seem remarkably certain of the duration, if I may say so.'

Anthony wanted to tell this nosey policeman that, towards the end, he'd been counting the days like a prisoner in a cell. But he decided that that would be unwise and remained silent.

'I take it you were both residing in London at the time?'

'Yes, inspector. In separate residences.'

'You were then a second-hand book dealer, I believe?'

'In a half-hearted sort of way. I'd just left teaching.'

'Where was that, sir?'

'Where was what?'

'The school you had been employed at?'

'Is that really relevant, inspector? It was an awfully long time ago.' Anthony shifted uneasily in his chair.

'Who's to know? We try to follow up all lines of enquiry.' He gave an insincere smile. 'The name of the school, Mr Metcalf?'

'Birch Cross Boys School, Horsham in Sussex.'

'Thank you, sir. Can we come now to your movements this week? In particular, can you tell us what you did on Thursday afternoon and evening? Say, from about 4.00pm.'

Anthony looked across at the embers in the fire and tried to marshal his activities of that day into the correct sequence.

'Let's see. Well, I closed the shop up just before 6.00p.m. Then I walked across to The Feathers Hotel to have a drink with a friend who works in Ludlow Market.'

'His name, if you please?'

'Terry Daniels.'

'Would you have a contact number to hand?'

Anthony fished his new mobile phone from his pocket, brought up Terry's details and slid the phone across the table for Rachel Tierney to take down the number.

'We parted company at round about 7.30p.m., I think. Then I

drove back here. Got my own supper as my wife was out, briefly watched *Question Time* and turned in at around 9.00p.m.'

'Were there any callers at the house that evening?'

'No, no-one.'

'Anyone ring you?'

'Nobody.'

'Did you speak to any passers-by or neighbours after you'd put your car in the garage?'

'No.'

'See anyone outside?'

Anthony suddenly remembered the figure standing in the lane. And in that same moment, knew who it was.

'Err, no. Nobody.'

He was distracted by a movement to his right. Rachel Tierney had leaned sideways in her chair, to reach down and release the two chrome clips on the top of her document box.

'Returning to your more recent contacts with Mrs Carlssen, sir. Did you ever visit her at the cottage she was renting at Bishop's Frome?'

'No I didn't.'

'Are you sure?'

'I wouldn't even know where it was, inspector.'

'Did you have any other form of contact with her there?'

'How do you mean?'

'Did you, for example, ever write to her there? A letter, perhaps... or a postcard?'

'Possibly.'

The West Indian detective flipped open the document box's lid and withdrew several plastic folders, which she placed on the table by her elbow. She slid the top one across to her superior.

As it passed in front of him, Anthony could clearly make out his own handwriting on a small pale blue envelope. The detective inspector swivelled the wallet through ninety degrees and then slid it back in front of Anthony.

'Would that be your handwriting on the envelope in the wallet, by any chance, sir?'

Anthony bravely attempted insouciance. 'Could be.'

'You'll see that the postmarked stamp shows that it was posted in Ludlow on 18th of August. Did you send Mrs Carlssen any sort of written communication on that day?'

'I really couldn't say for sure, inspector. It's possible that I dropped her a note from the shop – after she'd called in and we'd gone for a coffee.'

'Now, without removing the contents of the wallet, would you mind turning it over for me?'

Anthony turned the plastic folder over. Set behind the envelope was a small blue card – barely twice the size of a credit card – bearing some more of his handwriting. It was undated.

'Would you mind reading the message out, Mr Metcalf?'

Anthony took a long swig of water from the tumbler and cleared his throat. '"Last night was wonderful. We must do it again very soon."'

'And it's initialled "A", is it not?'

Anthony nodded. 'May I ask where you found the envelope?'

'One of my officers found it in an inside pocket of one of the victim's handbags, in her bedroom.'

'Well it may interest you to know, inspector, that although the envelope was posted in Ludlow less than 10 days ago, its contents – this little card...' he tapped it with an index finger '...is six years old!'

The senior police officer stretched out and retrieved the wallet. 'Are you suggesting, Mr Metcalf, that Mrs Carlssen swapped this card for the one which the envelope originally contained?'

'It looks very much like it, inspector. Because I can assure that I didn't write that note last week.'

'Why would Mrs Carlssen do that?'

'Search me.'

Benjamin signalled once more to the junior officer to pass him the next piece of evidence. From his vantage point, Anthony could see that the second wallet looked ominously as if it contained two long narrow airline tickets.

'According to one of the retained text messages on the late Mrs Carlssen's mobile phone...' the policeman looked down at a typed transcript '... she appears to have been planning to make a trip to the Canary Islands.'

'Yes, she did speak of it.'

'Accompanied by yourself, sir?'

'Certainly not! Although she had suggested it, I made it abundantly clear to her, on more than one occasion, that it was completely out of the question.'

Anthony heard the stealthy slither of the plastic wallet being pushed towards him by Detective Inspector Benjamin.

'These airline tickets would appear to contradict that, would they not, sir?' Benjamin's facial insinuation was dismissive.

Anthony glanced down. There were two Air France tickets, set inside the wallet one above the other, bearing the passenger names of "Mrs E. Carlssen" and "Mr A. Metcalf".

'May I ask where you found these?'

'One of my officers found them propped up on the mantelpiece in the lady's bedroom.'

Anthony shook his head despairingly. 'Look, inspector, I told her until I was blue in the face that I wasn't going. I'm sorry, but it's got nothing to do with me if this woman goes off and makes the booking.' He slid the folder away irritably, as if to indicate he wanted to have nothing more to do with it.

Benjamin seemed unfazed by the denial. He nodded to Miss

Tierney to pass him a third wallet. As it passed between the two detectives, Anthony could see that it was as a colour photo of a white tin can. When he saw the bright blue nozzle on top of the can, his heart sank. He knew it could only be a picture of the missing tin of weed killer.

Dave Benjamin cleared his throat, as if to deliver a sermon in church.

'Earlier in this interview, Mr Metcalf, you asked about the cause of Mrs Carlssen's death. And I informed you that we were awaiting a toxicology report, from our laboratories in Birmingham. However, initial – and as yet unconfirmed – reports suggest that Mrs Carlssen may have been poisoned. I stress "may".

'The photograph in front of you, sir, is of a half-litre can of an extremely noxious weed killer, which was found in the medicine cabinet of the bathroom at Honeysuckle Cottage. As yet, we have not checked any of the several sets of finger prints which are on the tin. However, from the label on the underside, we have been able to trace the retailer who sold the tin. It came from Williams in Ludlow. Their stock records show that the purchase was made on 20th of August; that it was paid for with a credit card; and according to the card issuer's records, that card is registered in your name at this address.

'So I must ask you, Mr Metcalf: have you purchased a can of weed killer from Williams in the last ten days?'

Anthony decided to brazen it out. 'As your painstaking research shows, inspector, I did indeed purchase a can of weed killer from Williams. It may well be the one in your photograph. And, as far as I'm aware, it's not against the law to buy weed killer to use in one's garden. However, three days after I purchased the tin – even before our gardener had had a chance to use it – it disappeared from our garage.'

'By "disappeared" I take it you mean it was stolen?'

'Those are your words not mine, inspector. I bought a tin of weed killer on a Thursday and by the following Tuesday it had vanished.'

'Where was it kept?'

'On a shelf at the back of our garage.'

'Is the garage kept locked?'

'No. I know it should be, but it makes access to the garage and a rear wash room easier for the gardener when we're not at home.'

'And at night?'

'I just pull the up-and-over door down.'

'What else went missing from your garage? The lawn mower, perhaps? Some power tools?'

'Nothing else.'

With thinly-disguised disbelief, Benjamin nodded across to his young note-taker. 'So a sneak thief helped himself to a can of weed killer – but nothing else?'

Anthony ignored the sarcasm and remained silent.

The inspector's mobile phone gave three rings. He looked at the screen and stood up, moving towards the entrance hall. 'Excuse me a moment.'

'Carry on Ted.'

The station sergeant asked: 'OK to talk?'

'Sure.'

'The toxicology report just came through. It's very thorough. In a nutshell: time of death was between 9.00pm and midnight yesterday. The weed killer was diluted 50:50 with champagne – hence the empty bottle found by the garden shed.'

'S'truth – what a cocktail!'

'Yeah. But this is the bit you're not going to like...'

'Go on.'

'There's only one set of prints on the champagne bottle.'

'And they are?'

'The victim's.'

'Certain?'

'One hundred per cent. The lab people removed the foil from the neck, in case it had been removed and replaced; they even dusted the punt.'

'The what?'

'The conical indentation on the underside of a champagne bottle. Thought you'd have known that, Dave, being the station's gourmet.'

Dave Benjamin cupped his hand around his phone and moved to the furthest end of the hallway. 'So from that we must conclude that the victim's assailant was wearing gloves.'

'Or it was self-administered.'

'Come again, Ted?'

'No prints but the victim's. Suppose the lady mixed herself the Glyphosate and champagne cocktail? It wouldn't be a first.'

'Well I'm bringing him in. We'll be with you within the hour.'

'Right ho, Dave.'

The long-case clock in the corner began its elaborate Whittington chime cycle for 10.00p.m.

'Do you have any further questions, inspector? It's awfully late and I really would like to prepare a light snack for my wife for when she returns, if you don't mind?'

'Nearly finished, sir. Right Rachel, where were we?'

Alongside the young detective sergeant's arm lay a small plastic pouch nestled inside the final wallet, with a hand-written luggage label attached to it by string. She slid it across to the senior officer. Benjamin kept its contents concealed under the palm of his hand.

'When two officers from Ludlow Station visited Florian's Restaurant this afternoon, Mr Metcalf, they interviewed the young waitress who had served you and Mrs Carlssen on the morning you took coffee together there. There was a receipt for your drinks and meal in Mrs Carlssen's bag, you see? ('These people certainly are thorough,' Anthony thought.)

'She gave my colleagues an approximate description of the

garments you were both wearing that day. Julia - that's the waitress in question - told them that she's pretty sure you were wearing a lightweight blue sports jacket.' He looked at Anthony for confirmation.

'Possibly, I really don't remember. What's your point, inspector?'

'My point, Mr Metcalf, is that I didn't see that jacket hanging on the coat rack in the hall when we came in.'

'So?'

'Before we leave, I would like to inspect it, sir, if I may. Is there anywhere else in the house that a blue sports jacket might be hanging?'

Anthony shrugged. 'As it's one of my items of casual wear – as opposed to "best" – it's probably hanging in the downstairs washroom at the back of the garage.'

'Would you mind fetching it, sir? There's just one small detail about it which we'd like to clear up. And then we'll be on our way.' The half-smile was menacing rather than friendly.

'Very well. I'll be right back.'

Anthony returned, with his old blue jacket draped over his arm. Benjamin and Tierney were now standing impassively at the table. The inspector was slowly fingering the mysterious plastic pouch, which he had now removed from the wallet.

'Would you mind placing the jacket on the table for us, please, Mr Metcalf?'

Anthony stretched his creased, much-loved blue jacket along the length of the table.

'Thank you, sir.' He momentarily glanced down at the small pouch in his hand. 'Now I haven't gone into the distressing details concerning the discovery today of Mrs Carlssen's body. Suffice it to say that she was found, not in the cottage, but in the garden. Crouched against a garden shed. My officers say that advanced rigor mortis had set in. Combined with the low air temperature last night, her body was effectively locked into a rigid position.

'A subsequent forensic examination of the cadaver in Birmingham revealed that this object...' he tossed the pouch across the table, to land in front of Anthony, 'was discovered clutched in the lady's right hand.'

Anthony looked down at a single red button, trapped inside the plastic pouch.

'As I think you can see, it is a small red button, probably from a jacket cuff. Rachel: please record that Mr Metcalf has been shown the button found in Mrs Carlssen's hand.'

He nodded at the garment which Anthony had laid on the table. 'Would you mind turning it over? So that we can all see the sleeve cuffs?'

Anthony slowly turned over the left arm, to reveal four small red buttons, in line at the base of the sleeve.

'And now the other one, if you wouldn't mind, sir.'

He flipped it over. There were only three buttons.

Ben the Sheltie leapt up excitedly as a car drew up.

A stunned Barbara was standing in the hallway. She wore a quilted black driving coat and her door keys hung at her side. She looked with disbelief at the frozen trio, staring down at Anthony's creased blue jacket draped across the dining table.

Rachel Tierney produced a dry cleaners' plastic jacket and began to carefully pack Anthony's jacket into it.

'Anthony Ellington Metcalf – I am arresting you on suspicion of the murder of Eva Carlssen, at Bishop's Frome in the County of Herefordshire. You are not obliged to say anything at this stage, but anything that you do say will be taken down and may be used in evidence against you at a later date.'

# XI

## *HMP Carding*

SEATED BETWEEN two young shirt-sleeved officers, Anthony Metcalf stared disbelievingly ahead through the windscreen of the police car, as it made its way northwards out of Ludlow. Apart from the occasional indecipherable squawk from the two-way radio, there was silence in the saloon. The driver leant across and clicked a switch on the dashboard. 'Ludlow?'

'Roger.'

'What's our ETA at Carding, please?'

'Fourteen-forty-five.'

'Wilco.'

Such was the speed of the awful incidents crowding in on Anthony's life, that he found it difficult to comprehend that it was less than 15 hours since he had been escorted from his own home by two detectives, to face a second interrogation at Ludlow Police Station. Then a miserable, sleepless night in a smelly cell, followed at break-neck speed, by a special sitting, before three local magistrates, at which he had been committed for trial, charged with murder.

The white Vauxhall veered to the left at the first roundabout on the outskirts of Craven Arms and proceeded along a densely-wooded back road. After slowing to pass through the tiny hamlet of Clifford, the police car continued westwards for another mile.

A small directional road sign, with an arrow pointing to the left, alerted Anthony that they were approaching their destination: HMP CARDING. The car slowed and turned into a narrow lane.

Tall perimeter security fences soon appeared at the verge sides. The lane reduced to a single carriageway, interspersed by passing bays. Suddenly, a giant clock tower hove into view above a line of chestnut trees.

The police car slowed to a crawl, stopping directly in front of a wide, round-headed stone arch framing a huge pair of steel entrance gates, incongruously painted with black and yellow chevron stripes. Incised in Roman capitals around the archway was the clue to this Victorian building's original purpose: SANITORIUM.

The four policemen stared ahead without speaking. The driver checked his wristwatch: 2.43p.m. Nobody appeared from within the prison complex and the gates remained firmly shut.

Through the car's glass roof, Anthony gazed upwards at the clock tower, whose dark red brickwork was decorated with regularly-spaced bands of cream glazed tiles. The impressive structure was capped by a green, copper-clad roof and the hour and minute hands on the clock face were missing.

Two minutes later, the silence was broken by the shrill sound of a warning claxon, as the steel entrance gates automatically rolled sideways. Beyond the arch, a huge rectangular paved inner courtyard was revealed, overlooked by four identical, three-storey wings. Small gothic-pointed windows, framed by sandstone dressings, ran along the facades. Above them, steeply-pitched slate roofs were punctuated by tiny attic gables.

Down the centre of the courtyard was a narrow band of old cobbles, along which the Vauxhall drove, coming to a halt opposite a dark blue wooden entrance door marked: HMP CARDING RECEPTION.

One of Anthony's two rear-seat companions stepped into the courtyard to let him out, lightly clasping his elbow. The second officer joined him on his other side. The front seat passenger, clutching a blue clipboard under his arm, approached the entrance door and knocked. The driver remained at the wheel.

'This way, Metcalf.'

The space into which they stepped was as far removed as it was possible to be from a conventional reception area. Devoid of all furniture - save for three steel-framed chairs with black vinyl seats - the square room was dominated by a long white counter, guarded by a prison officer. Looking at the visitor, he said: 'Approach the desk!'

As he stood before this unsmiling man, Anthony realised that the prison official was a good 18" taller and must therefore be standing on some sort of raised platform.

'Anthony Ellington Metcalf?'

'Yes, sir.'

'From now on, you are "Metcalf 741". Understood?'

'Yes, sir.'

The guard reached below the counter and withdrew a grey plastic tray. Tattooed along his outstretched forearm was a large anchor, entwined by a voluptuous mermaid. He banged the tray down on the counter top.

'Remove everything from your pockets and place them in this tray. Then take all your clothes off and put them in there too.' He gestured with a sideways nod of his head to a glazed door beyond the counter. 'When you're undressed, go into that room for a strip search, then return here in your uniform. You can sign for your belongings before you're taken to your cell.'

The bodily examination was every bit as humiliating as Anthony had imagined it would be, particularly as it was roughly undertaken by two muscular male officers, one of whom smelt strongly of tobacco.

After slipping into a pair of grey cotton boxer shorts, a dark blue long-sleeved pullover and a light grey track suit bottom, he walked barefooted into the reception area, carrying a pair of grey trainers. His three escorts from Ludlow had gone.

'Listen carefully. Meals are at 8, 12 and 6. Lock-up is at 9.00p.m. Communal showers are Mondays, Wednesdays and Fridays. Exercise in the yard is every Sunday from 10.00 to 11.30a.m., weather permitting. At all other times you remain in your cell. If you need anything, you stand in the cell doorway and call: "Guard". No time-wasting trivia. Understood?'

'Yes, sir.'

'Any questions?'

'Am I permitted to make a phone call?'

'Who to, the wife?'

'No, my solicitor actually.'

'Wasn't he at your committal this morning?'

'No, unfortunately he had to attend his son's school Speech Day.'

'Funny sort of brief you've got yourself, Metcalf. I'd have thought a murder charge would take priority over a kid's Speech Day.'

'I agree. But I need to ask him what arrangements he's made for my defence counsel.'

''Struth, you're cutting it a bit fine, ain't you?'

'How do you mean, sir?'

'When d'you suppose your case is coming up?'

'They didn't say at the committal. A week or two, I suppose.'

The officer reached across to the end of the counter and withdrew a thin sheath of official-looking papers. 'Well, let me enlighten you, Metcalf 741. "Shrewsbury Crown Court. Monday 31 August 2015. Before Judge Sir William Roxburgh. The Queen v Metcalf." He slid the papers back. 'Day after tomorrow. 10.00a.m.'

Anthony's heart sank into his prison-issue trainers. Feeling his body begin to shake, he reached forward and gripped the edge of the desk. His face was drained.

'Sorry to be the bearer of bad tidings.' The apology sounded genuine. 'Want to sit down before you're taken to your cell?'

Anthony shook his head glumly. 'No, I'll be OK.'

'Very well.' The guard picked up the phone on the desk and tapped in a couple of numbers. 'Metcalf 741 to his cell.' He replaced the receiver.

A younger, fresher-faced guard arrived to escort Anthony down a long dimly-lit corridor. The unadorned walls, painted in an institutional colour scheme of magnolia and chocolate brown, on one side looked out onto the rectangular exercise yard, with the opposite wall of the corridor containing cell doorways.

The officer paused by the eighth door opening and gestured for Anthony to go in. His cell was less than four metres by three metres, with about one-sixth of the space given over to a stainless steel wc and washbasin. A towel, a small bar of soap, a rug and a pillow were laid out on a steel-framed bunk bed. The one minor compensation was the natural light flooding into the cell from the far end, through a gothic window, which framed an enticing view of rolling Shropshire farmland.

The guard paused in the doorway for a moment. 'Supper will be at 6.00p.m.,' then walked off, his keys banging against his trouser leg. Anthony stretched out on the unmade bed and soon nodded off.

He remained unconscious for over an hour, to be awoken by a trundling sound echoing down the main corridor. After a few moments it stopped, followed by distant voices. Then the mechanical rhythm resumed and grew louder. He looked towards the open cell door. From the direction of the reception suite, a dark-stained wooden trolley appeared. It had green rubber wheels and around 70 or 80 paperbacks ranged neatly along its four angled shelves. It came to a halt in the doorway and an elderly, round-faced West Indian man stood beaming behind this miniature mobile library. Placing his hands across the top shelf, he asked proprietarily: 'Good afternoon. Can I interest you in any reading matter?'

Anthony sat up. 'Good afternoon to you. Yes, possibly. What have you got there?'

'All sorts, my friend. Thrillers, westerns...' he picked up a fat volume '... historical fiction. Mrs Mantel — now there's a fine writer! Bodice rippers — though our ones are pretty tame. Sports biographies? I don't imagine you'll be wanting to get stuck into a murder mystery, somehow!'

'Let me try Hilary Mantel, would you?'

'Certainly.' He took a pencil from his pocket and scribbled a date inside the cover, before handing it to Anthony. 'There you go — a fortnight.'

'Thanks'. He flicked through the opening pages of *Wolf Hall*. The man had now stepped into the cell. He was well past 60, Anthony guessed, with his curly white hair neatly trimmed. The benevolent appearance was completed by gold-framed half-moon spectacles, perched mid-way down his nose. He had a professional air about him.

'So what are you in for?' Anthony asked the visitor.

'I ain't in for nothin', my friend and neither are you! We've been remanded, awaiting trial. You for murder, and me for embezzlement.'

'Embezzlement, eh? Big amounts?'

'Huge, man. Awesome. Nine counts, totalling £850,000. And all syphoned off out of my clients' accounts by my talented young Slovenian PA, Vanessa. In whose mouth butter wouldn't even melt!'

'I see. Leaving you to face the music. And where is she now?'

'Long gone, man; long gone. Somewhere in the Caribbean, last I heard.'

'Has your case started yet?'

'Started twice and adjourned twice. Once because HMRC sent the wrong papers to court, and once because my brief went down with the measles. Seems there's one law for the wealthy and privileged, and one for the likes of us.

'Remember Bopal? The Indian gas tragedy of 1984, which eventually caused the deaths of 15,000 people? Did Union Carbide's boss Warren Anderson ever go to jail? No he did NOT. He died in a Florida nursing home. How many UK bankers do you suppose are presently behind bars for the LIBOR interest rate-rigging scandal, for which UK banks were fined £2-billion? Currently just one!' He shook his head sadly. 'Man, that ain't what I calls justice.'

'So how long have you been on remand?'

'Two months. So you should thank your lucky stars your case is coming up on Monday morning.'

'I don't quite see it that way, I'm afraid. Especially as I haven't even met my defence counsel yet.'

The prison book minder did a clicking noise with his tongue against his teeth and winced. 'My, you're cuttin' it a bit fine, ain't you?'

'Exactly the words the officer in reception used this afternoon, when I was admitted.'

'Still, you're up before Roxburgh.'

'Come again?'

The black man nonchalantly straightened the books on the cart's top shelf. 'His Honour Sir William Roxburgh. Best beak on the Midland Circuit. "Firm-but-fair Roxburgh", he's known as.'

'Parker!' a voice called from the distance. 'Books wanted on the North Wing! Get a move on!'

The man shrugged, gave a half-smile and went to the doorway. 'Be right there boss,' he called then returned to Anthony's cell and sat down on the end of the bunk bed beside him. 'And the other thing you've got to be thankful for is that we ain't banged up in The Dana.'

'What's The Dana?'

'What was The Dana, you mean. Only the most vile and fetid cess pit of a penitentiary anywhere on this sceptered isle. Most over-crowded and with the highest suicide rate. Ever read A. E. Houseman?'

'Yes, when I was an English master. But that was a long time ago.'

'*A Shropshire Lad?*'

'Yes.'

'Well read it again, my friend, when you can. Houseman will tell you what conditions were like in Shrewsbury's Dana Gaol.'

'Parker! Books – North Wing. NOW!' The summons was bellowed this time.

'On my way, boss; on my way.' With a wink and a cheery grin, the old man pushed his noisy trolley off down the corridor.

In the hour which remained before his evening meal was due to arrive, Anthony resolved to immerse himself in Hilary Mantel's Tudor drama. He was quickly absorbed by the writer's expert scene setting of Thomas Cromwell's lavish household, when he suddenly became aware that he was being watched from the cell doorway.

A tall, slim dark-haired young woman, wearing crisp blue jeans and a long-sleeved pale blue cotton jumper, was studying him. She gave an attractive smile. She was clearly under 30 and the only indication of her role in the prison hierarchy was the white clerical collar projecting above the neckline of her top. A large bunch of keys hung from a green sash around her waist.

'Anthony, I believe. How are we settling in?'

'Fair-to-middling, thank you vicar..., padre..., chaplain.'

'Ann will do fine. I'm Ann Slocombe, Prison Chaplain. Would you like to talk before your supper arrives?'

'What I would really like, Ann – if it comes within your jurisdiction – is to visit a place of worship. Does such a thing exist here in Carding?'

'It most certainly does. We have a very beautiful chapel at the far end of this corridor, on the East Wing. But you'll have to be accompanied.'

'By whom?'

'If Reception approves your request, I can take you.'

'I'd like that very much, Ann. So what do I have to do?'

'Leave everything to me. And place your trust in God. I'll return after your supper tray has been collected, then hopefully we can visit the Maitland Chapel together.'

Dusk was adding a sombre gloom to the corridor outside when the chaplain returned an hour-and-a-half later. She stood smiling in the doorway. 'Ready?' she asked brightly.

Putting aside his book, Anthony jumped up enthusiastically. 'So our request was approved?'

She smiled back at the prisoner. 'Of course! Malcolm's OK. It's just that he looks a bit fearsome – but underneath that veneer, he's an old softie! Follow me,'

They swiftly navigated their way through two sets of barred steel corridor doors, with Ann Slocombe nimbly selecting the correct key both times. As they rounded the corner onto the East Wing, directly ahead of them, bathed in a dull half-light, Anthony was startled to see a tableau of two motionless figures. He hesitated, unable to fully assimilate the strange vision, and halted in disbelief. Grasping his elbow comfortingly, the chaplain whispered: 'Don't be afraid, Anthony - it's only our benefactor, Sir Charles Maitland. It's made of marble.'

Slowly, the vision came into focus, like an ever-enlarging movie zoom lens. Now the bas-relief tableau was life-sized and eerily lifelike. The scene depicted a seated male figure in a Victorian frock coat, slumped back and seemingly half-asleep. Above him, with her right hand raised towards Heaven, stood the Angel of Death, her other hand rested on his shoulder. Books were scattered across a table, with an expired hour glass in the foreground.

Ann Slocombe, in her enthusiasm to reach the chapel, had gone ahead several paces. She moved back, to stand alongside Anthony. 'I know – it's a bit macabre, isn't it?'

'What is it? I can see it's beautifully crafted – Carrara, I'd say. But what exactly is going on?'

'It depicts the death throes of Sir Charles Maitland, whose individual generosity built this place – once the foremost sanatorium dedicated to the treatment of consumption, otherwise known as tuberculosis. There used to be over 200 patients here, many of them terminal.'

'Hence the name over the entrance arch?'

'Exactly. It was known as Maitland's Sanatorium for over a century. But modern political correctness being what it is, this worthy edifice had to be transmogrified by officialdom into HMP CARDING.' She nodded at the statue. 'Fortunately, old Sir Charles lives on.'

She moved forwards. 'Actually this isn't a bad nick. We haven't had a suicide in nearly a year. Let's go inside, shall we?'

Just as the death throes of Sir Charles Maitland had halted Anthony in his tracks with disbelief, so the first glimpse of the interior of the former sanatorium's chapel of worship lifted his heart with joyous thanksgiving. Ann Slocombe gently nudged his elbow, as she swung open the narrow stained glass door.

Gingerly, he stepped into a perfectly-formed cruciform-shaped jewel box. High above the tiny black marble altar, a red octagonal chancel lamp suffused the chapel's interior with a gentle flickering crimson light. The high vaulted ceiling was lined with gilded scallop shells, iridescent in the light. Mahogany prayer desks, with ivory inlay and velvet crimson kneelers, flanked the altar, in the centre of which was a heavily-gilded tabernacle. The lace-edged altar cloth was embroidered: SIR CHARLES MAITLAND Bt 1808-87. The nave itself had two single pews, separated by the central aisle, seating no more than eight worshippers. Anthony knelt at the altar rail to pray.

Ten minutes later he stepped outside the tiny chapel, gently pulling the door closed behind him. The prison chaplain was seated on a window ledge. 'Thank you so much, Ann, I really appreciated that.'

'Yes, I sensed that this afternoon. Let's hope you sleep soundly.'

'I'm sure I will.'

Like Gustave Doré's Newgate prisoners, Carding's inmates shuffled lethargically around the prison's rectangular inner courtyard on their weekly exercise.

There was no order or regimentation to this desultory brigade, sloping along two, three and four abreast; mumbling, cursing or softly humming. Occasional scraps of paper would be exchanged or cigarette buts passed around clandestinely. The handless clock looked down from the top of the Italianate tower, as if reminding the prisoners: "Time stands still here."

Tiny black plastic loudspeakers were set high upon the walls, at the four corners of the courtyard. Along with the roof level security lighting, they were the only non-Victorian anachronisms on view. Suddenly, the speakers crackled into life. "Metcalf 741 to Reception. Metcalf 741 to Reception. Immediately."

Three prisoners, walking directly in front of Anthony (including Herbert Parker), swung round to look at him. The old man nodded towards the westernmost corner of the yard and whispered: 'Get a move on, man – that'll be that idle brief of yours!'

The wise Barbadian's prediction was correct – though as a crestfallen Anthony was to discover, as he stood to attention in front of the reception counter – Gerald Stewart was calling by phone from Ludlow and not attending in person. He took the call in front of the duty officer.

'Listen, I'm most frightfully sorry I couldn't get up there yesterday. Fact is, Harry's Speech Day didn't finish until 5.00p.m. and then it was drinks and canapés in the Headmaster's house. In the end, Celia and I didn't get back until gone 9.00p.m. I gather you're committed to Shrewsbury Crown Court for tomorrow. I'll be coming up, of course; I'll probably drive up with Barbara...'

Anthony ended the diatribe of excuses and trivia. 'Gerald – what have you done about my defence? Where's my bloody brief, for Christ's sake? It's Sunday morning and I still don't know who's going to defend me!'

'All taken care of, old man.'

The duty officer looked on with mild amusement.

'What's that supposed to mean?'

'My secretary's been in touch with the Bristol chambers we usually use in criminal cases. Their clerk recommended a Miss Clare Miller, so Emilie – that's my secretary – emailed her all the necessary background documents on Saturday afternoon, after your committal.'

'But where is she?'

'Where's who – Emilie?'

'No, you wally - this Clare Miller! Am I supposed to communicate with her from Shropshire by mental telepathy?'

'Ah yes. Well, we had a slight logistical problem today. You see, Clare was going to travel up from Bristol by train this morning, but Network Rail decided to carry out some engineering works between Hereford and Shrewsbury. So no trains.'

'Bloody brilliant! For sheer incompetence, Gerald, you certainly take the biscuit!'

'*Nil desperandum* old man.'

Hoping that the eaves-dropping duty officer might be sympathetic to his plight, Anthony put his hand over the receiver's mouthpiece. 'I don't suppose you'd have any idea what time they'll be taking me to Shrewsbury Crown Court in the morning, would you sir?'

Without looking up, the guard replied: 'Court usually sits at 10.00a.m, so you'll be delivered to the court's cell complex by 8.30a.m. The van will be leaving just before eight, I'd say.'

'Thank you, I'm most grateful. Gerald – are you still there? Right, now listen carefully, because I'm not going to repeat this. Get on to this Clare Miller now, as soon as this call has ended. Tell her she's to be at Shrewsbury Crown Court by 8.30a.m. tomorrow morning. Got that?'

'Bit early isn't it, old man?'

'I don't care if she has to hire a fucking helicopter – because it'll be your poxy office that'll be paying for it! And if she's not there in person, I'll be sending a stiff letter on cardboard to the Law Society, you slap head! Goodbye,' Resisting the temptation to slam the receiver down, Anthony simply handed it back to the guard with a half-smile. 'Thank you, sir.'

The guard smiled and raised his eyebrows enquiringly. 'Friend of yours?'

'Ex friend.'

Anthony walked out of the reception suite feeling a lot better and rejoined the exercise column.

Always a light sleeper in summer, Anthony awoke at 5.30a.m. He intended to skip breakfast (though he yearned for a life-enhancing double espresso coffee) as he wanted to be ready in good time to travel to Shrewsbury in the armoured police van, which he was confident would be parked out in the central yard within the hour.

The journey northwards was uneventful. Seated on facing rows of slatted wooden benches, the six prisoners remained silent. With no sight of the passing landscape through the one-way glass of the van's windows, the journey was monotonous. The diesel engine's revolutions, together with occasional slowing motions at junctions and roundabouts, were the only clues to the vehicle's transition from their rural redoubt to the outskirts of the large market town. And its seat of justice.

'Passing the Abbey now, lads,' whispered an experienced old lag. 'In about three minutes, get ready to duck.'

The van halted. Instructions were exchanged and as it inched forward over the traffic flow plates, the cry went up: 'Duck!' The simultaneous flashes of half-a-dozen Press cameras, pushed against the prison van's windows, vividly illuminated the gloomy interior. While his companions had all slumped forward, Anthony only had time to shield his eyes with one arm from the invasive glare.

The van slowly descended a steep ramp, then drew to a halt. The engine was switched off. Now it was pitch black in the back of the van. 'Come on you lazy sods,' whispered one of the old lags, 'let's get some fresh air.'

'What time's your meet with your brief?' came a knowing voice from the bench opposite.

'Eight-thirty,' he volunteered to the invisible stranger.

'We're early. It's only 8.15a.m. You're quids in.'

Another voice joined the discussion. 'An hour-and-three-quarters to work out his defence? Blimey, Mickey, the Yorkshire Ripper wouldn't have needed that long!'

Anthony felt a consoling hand grip his thigh. 'You'll be fine, mate. Good luck!' Two minutes later the van's rear doors were swung open.

'Down the steps and inside the cell complex. And no talking.'

Shrewsbury Crown Court's holding cells, beneath the two court rooms, were spotlessly tidy. Anthony's cell comprised a narrow bunk bed, a melamine-topped table and two upright chairs. High up in the ceiling, shafts of natural light came from a grid of tempered-glass blocks.

Less than ten minutes after his arrival, Anthony was startled by a loud thump on the cell's closed metal door. 'Metcalf 741: visitor. Stand back from the door by your bunk.' Keys clanged and the door was thrust open.

Standing in front of a uniformed police officer was a tall, dark-haired young woman in her mid-20s. In her black leather court shoes she was almost as tall as Anthony. She wore a high-collared white silk blouse with black buttons and a three-quarter length black pleated skirt. She clutched a bulging black leather briefcase under one arm and offered her free hand. 'Good morning. I'm Clare Miller, your barrister, Mr Metcalf.'

Anthony gave her a big smile. 'Am I pleased to see you!'

Anthony and Clare seated themselves at the table. The young

woman industriously unpacked her briefcase, forming the papers into three stacks. Countless yellow Post-It slips projected from the ends of the documents. She took off her watch and placed it on the table.

'OK. We've got one-and-a-half hours. Probably more, as there's to be a bail plea from a Latvian shoplifter (you must have come in with him on the van), which our judge has agreed to hear first, as the CPS has had to bring a translator up from London specially. So we might have as much as two hours.'

Anthony stared disconsolately at the paper mountain in front of them. It would take him all day to even read them – and even longer to understand their contents. The young barrister continued in her confident manner. 'Tell me: how much do you know about Crown Court procedure?'

'Precious little.'

'You are the defendant – effectively the person the Crown is accusing of murder. I am your advocate. I speak for you. I have to convince the jury of your innocence. The prosecuting barrister, who will open the case, will produce evidence he believes will convince the jury you killed Mrs Carlssen. The judge is the umpire. Simple as that.'

Still gazing at the paperwork, Anthony gave a wry smile. In less than 60 words, fluently delivered in under a minute, this formidable young advocate had summarised the court's procedure.

She split one of the piles of papers open with her fingernail, withdrawing a single sheet marked "Exhibits 6&7". 'Now I have to ask you one crucially important question, Anthony – OK if I call you Anthony?'

'Certainly. What is it?'

'It's not whether you killed Mrs Carlssen; I know you didn't. It is this: did you write that "Last night was wonderful..." card?'

'Yes.'

'When?'

'Six years ago.'

Clare Miller smiled and replaced the sheet in the stack. 'Good, that's all I needed to know!

Now I'm reasonably confident about the blue card the message was written on, but the red cuff button remains a worry. The prosecution is going to produce an expert witness from Italy. It's always a bad sign when the CPS lashes out on foreign travel expenses.'

They worked meticulously through the key court documents and depositions, including transcripts of Anthony's two police interviews. After about an hour, a low-noted buzzer sounded from the far end of the passageway outside the cell. "Court Number One is now in session. Judge Roxburgh presiding," came the announcement over the tannoy.

'That'll be the shoplifter. I'd better go and get ready. Any questions?'

'Any tips on how I should deport myself in court?'

'Excellent question, Anthony! I wish more of my clients would ask that.' She stood up and began returning the documents to her briefcase, then clicked its chrome clips shut.

'You will be seated at the back of the court. The dock is a rather unfriendly structure – a glass box, in effect. I will be standing in front of you, but with my back to you. Prosecuting counsel will be on my right. You will be in full sight of the judge, the jury box and the witness stand. So all eyes will be upon you. Sit up straight at all times; whatever you do, don't slump forwards dejectedly. Don't make eye contact with any of the jurors – not even the pretty girlie ones – and only respond to eye contact from Judge Roxburgh if he directly addresses you. OK with that?'

'What about when I go in the witness box?'

'We'll talk about that tomorrow.'

Anthony ruefully reflected that Clare's exposition of court etiquette had taken twice as long to explain as her summary of its procedure.

There was a loud bang on the cell door, followed by the all-too-familiar rattle of keys. A woman police officer stood in the doorway. 'Miss Miller – Judge Roxburgh would like to see you in his chambers.'

The two women departed, though the cell door remained open. Shortly after, from along the corridor came the words Anthony had been dreading to hear: "Put up Anthony Metcalf." A young police officer in a white shirt was standing outside his cell.

The two men walked, single file, along the dark passageway. After about twenty paces, Anthony paused at the bottom of a flight of wooden steps that lead straight upwards. A simple whispered command came in his ear. 'Go up the steps.'

He grasped the handrail and started his ascent. Looking upwards, towards the brightly-lit court above, he assessed that there were probably two dozen steps to ascend. But half-way up, he lost his nerve and faltered, grasping the other handrail for stability. Two deep intakes of breath, then upwards to the dock. Behind him, he could hear his guard's keys banging against the side of the stairwell.

A bewildered Anthony stepped out onto a rectangular boarded platform measuring some five metres square. There was a row of vinyl-covered chairs along the back - doubtless for multiple-defendant cases, he reasoned. But this dock was not as he had imagined it would be. This was no mahogany-panelled Regency chicken coop; nor a wire-caged box from Cairo; nor even a civilised row of unscreened cushioned benches from Nuremberg. Shrewsbury Crown Court's dock was, as Clare Miller had warned, a glass-sided box, with tall thick slabs of armour-plated glass stretching up to a secure, wire mesh ceiling.

The body of the court was empty, save for two female ushers distributing court documents to the lawyers' desks. Anthony looked to his jailer for guidance. The young officer nodded towards the row of chairs. Anthony chose the second from the end and sat down. A plastic beaker of water was placed by his feet, then the guard took his seat at the opposite end of the row, directly in front of the locked door at the rear of the dock. Both men sat in silence, staring ahead.

Created in the in the 1960s, Shrewsbury's Crown Court was an amalgam of the traditional English court layout, overlaid with the pioneering modernism which had flowed from the seminal Festival of Britain. A paradigm for the modern face of jurisprudence. A multi-tiered windowless box (natural light was only admitted via a large square frosted glass rooflight), clad entirely in maple wood.

The judge's raised bench was flanked by two massive book stacks, containing leather-bound legal volumes, with a tall white marble screen (with the Royal Coat of Arms incised in gold) set directly behind a high-backed chair. Beneath this bench was the Clerk to the Court's desk.

To the judge's immediate right was the double-tiered jury box, comprising two rows of blue cushioned seats with desks. The witness stand was set at the judge's left-hand side and beyond it were two long rows of vinyl-covered benches, for lawyers and members of the Press.

The black-robed clerk left his desk and approached the door to the jury room, rapping on it twice. The door opened and the jury of five women and seven men filed nervously out and took their seats along the two benches. Two of the more elderly men wore suits and ties, while nearly everyone else wore casual summer clothes. One young Asian man and a smartly-attired, middle-aged Japanese lady were the only non-Caucasians.

'The court will rise,' ordered the clerk as Judge Sir William Roxburgh entered, cutting a distinguished figure in his long gown and full wig. The amber sash of the Midland Circuit was draped over his left shoulder. He nodded to the clerk and to the two advocates who stood below him.

A movement behind Anthony's left shoulder suggested that the public was being admitted to the public gallery: four long rows of red vinyl-covered benches, stretching across the back of the courtroom. The arrivals shuffled in, half-curious and half-embarrassed at coming to witness the spectacle. At the far end, Anthony caught sight of old Mr Williams, the proprietor of the ironmongers where he had purchased the weed killer. And was that really Terry's ex-wife Tina, dressed in an outfit more suited to Lady's Day at Ascot, sitting behind him?

From the furthest public door, Barbara entered. She was dressed entirely in black, wearing the same black fur-collared woollen coat she had worn to Anthony's father's funeral. Behind her followed a joyously-colourful Stephenie, clad in a figure-hugging two-piece summer outfit, which might have been designed for her by Henri Matisse himself. Dutifully taking up the rear was officer-cadet-to-be Tim Nugent. He gestured to the two women to take seats directly behind the dock, but Barbara declined, opting instead to sit behind Tina and the ironmonger. True to form, Anthony's solicitor Gerald Stewart managed to make a late arrival. Two shabbily dressed journalists slipped into the Press benches moments before the judge invited the suave-looking Crown counsel, Jeffrey Hughes, to open the case for the prosecution.

'Mr Hughes?'

'Thank you, your honour. Members of the jury, the case before you today – though drastically serious, since it involves the death of an innocent woman – is simple and straightforward. Ample evidence will be presented to show that the accused, Anthony Metcalf, was responsible for the death of Mrs Eva Carlssen.' With his slicked back dark hair, tall angular build and square shoulders, the prosecuting barrister reminded Anthony of the Spanish film actor Antonio Banderas. His clearly-enunciated delivery was almost haughty.

'Your honour, I propose to call only four witnesses, the first of whom is the lead investigator in this murder inquiry: Detective Inspector David Benjamin.' The inspector climbed up into the witness box.

The Hughes-Benjamin examination was predictably thorough, with no forensic stone left unturned. It lasted well over an hour, slowed by the difficulty two of the younger jurors had in following the texts of the typed transcripts of Benjamin's interviews with Anthony. Jeffrey Hughes sat down, well satisfied with his examination of the taciturn policeman.

Clare Miller looked at her watch: 11.10a.m. Too early for lunch, but just about the time when Judge Roxburgh usually needed his mid-morning double espresso. The old man gave her an avuncular smile. 'Miss Miller?'

'Thank you, your honour.' She turned slowly to face the detective. 'Inspector Benjamin, how many times did you visit the defendant's home – Kynaston Barn – in the course of your enquiries?'

Benjamin decided to waffle. 'I interviewed the defendant twice; once at his home and then later at Ludlow Police Station. Transcripts of both interviews are before the court, madam.' The "madam" was unnecessarily elongated, in the patronising style of a restaurant head waiter.

Clare looked up imploringly at the judge. 'I do apologise. That wasn't what I meant, inspector. How many times did you interview Mr Metcalf in his own home?'

Benjamin was on the back foot now, but couldn't see the flight of the ball. 'Err, only the once.'

Clare left a long pause before delivering her googly. 'But I understand that, accompanied by Detective Sergeant Tierney, you visited the property on the Saturday morning, shortly before the committal proceedings.'

Benjamin stared down at the bible he had given the oath on. 'Err, that is correct.'

'And yet there is no record of this visit before the court. Why is this, inspector?'

Benjamin looked for help from the bench.

'Miss Miller – where are we going?' asked the judge. His double espresso was now calling him urgently to his chambers.

'Your honour, I wish to establish why this senior investigating officer found it necessary to re-visit the defendant's home only two hours before the magistrates' committal court was due to sit, that is all.'

'Then I think this would be an appropriate moment to have a short adjournment.' He nodded down to his clerk. 'We will reconvene in 20 minutes.'

'The court will rise!'

At the resumption, Dave Benjamin was all padded up and ready to face the hostile bowling.

'Will you tell the court which parts of Kynaston Barn you inspected?'

'When?'

'On the Saturday morning, before committal.'

'Mainly the garage.'

'By "mainly the garage" can we take it that you mean "only the garage"?'

'Yes, ma'am; only the garage.'

'Thank you. And what were you looking for, inspector?'

'Err, evidence that one or other of the defendant's cars may have been used to drive to Bishop's Frome.'

Clare had the picture and the judge did too. But she left a slight pause, in order for the implication of the inspector's answer to be absorbed by the jury.

'Because – and forgive me if I appear to be acting like an amateur sleuth here – because you wanted to check the treads on the tyres of Mr Metcalf's two cars, to try to trace evidence of gravel chippings that might match the gravel samples which you had taken from the drive in front of Honeysuckle Cottage?'

'Something along those lines, yes ma'am,' the inspector grudgingly agreed.

'And?'

'And what?'

'And what were your findings after examining the cars? Where is Exhibit 999, inspector? The little plastic sachet of tell-tale gravel chippings removed from the Metcalfs' garage.'

The bowling was too hostile. Benjamin decided to lapse into police gobbledegook. 'In the limited time frame available, ma'am, my sergeant and I were unable to verify whether the said vehicles had contributed to the detected crime at Bishop's Frome.'

'In other words – and for the benefit of the jury – you found nothing. And you are therefore unable to produce any evidence that either of the defendant's cars were driven to Honeysuckle Cottage, Bishop's Frome?'

'Err, no, ma'am.'

'No further questions, your honour.'

Jeffrey Hughes next made a reasonably competent job of going through the Birmingham police laboratory's forensic report, relating to the quantities of Glyphosate found in the victim's digestive system. The jury was left in little doubt that Eva Carlssen had been poisoned, though by whose hand neither lawyer was prepared to vouchsafe.

After lunch, the forensic report was followed by the evidence of Harold Chadwick, the ironmongers' assistant who had sold Anthony the weed killer. Then after a short mid-afternoon adjournment, Jeffrey Hughes called Julia Bridgewater, the waitress who had served Anthony and Eva on their visit to Florian's Restaurant. Concluding his short questioning, Hughes sat down.

'Would you describe the defendant's manner towards Mrs Carlssen as hostile?' Clare Miller asked the young woman.

'On no, madam.'

'Amicable?'

The waitress weighed up the word. 'Yes, I'd say that covers it.'

'But nothing more?'

'How d'you mean, madam?'

'Well, did they hold hands, for example?'

'Oh no, madam; nothing like that. Mind, for part of the time I was in the kitchen fetching their order.'

'Quite so. So would you say, Miss Bridgewater, that these two people gave the impression of old friends, just meeting up for a coffee together?'

'Yes, I'd say so.'

'Just friends?'

'Yes.'

'Close friends?'

The girl paused and frowned. 'No, madam, just friends.'

'Who paid the bill?'

'Well Mr Metcalf was about to pay, but the lady brushed it aside. So Mr Metcalf left the tip.'

'And did you see them leave Florian's?'

'Err, no madam. I got called to serve a customer at the back of the restaurant, just as they were leaving.'

Clare nodded with satisfaction and sat down.

After Julia Bridgewater had left the witness stand, Judge Roxburgh leant forward to whisper to the clerk, who nodded, then turned towards the jury. 'I propose to rise early today, ladies and gentlemen, once the prosecution has called its last witness for the day. Mr Hughes?'

As the prosecuting barrister rose, Anthony's escort was changed, with a young policewoman joining him in the dock. She sat beside him. He turned to look over his shoulder and was disappointed to see that Barbara and Stephenie had left, though stalwart Tim Nugent remained at his post.

The last witness of the afternoon was Honeysuckle Cottage's housekeeper, Jenny Preece. The elderly cleaning lady's faltering evidence contributed little to the case, hindered by Jeffrey Hughes' patronising manner. With the aid of the illuminated video screens set in front of the witness stand and the jury box, he attempted to guide the old lady through the cottage's rooms. At one point, she was convinced that a scale plan of the kitchen was the first floor bathroom.

'Perhaps I could take you outside?' he suggested.

As he pressed a button on his desk, the screens went black, to be immediately followed by a grainy time-stamped colour image of a lop-sided garden shed. Everyone in the courtroom took a moment to assimilate the significance of the picture which the barrister had brought up onto the screens.

Against the wood-boarded side of the old shed, a large pile of rubbish – including a threadbare mattress – had been dumped. A blue-and-white striped police ribbon was stretched in front of the outhouse. Clearly visible at the bottom of the picture was an empty champagne bottle and beside it – sticking out from beneath the pile of black detritus, was a stark white arm and a clenched fist.

Jenny Preece screamed in horror at seeing this dreadful sight again. The clerk jumped to his feet and the judge raised his right arm angrily, indicating to Hughes to get rid of the offending picture. A policewoman stepped up into the witness box to comfort the cleaning lady, as the jury looked on in disbelief. The judge and the clerk conferred. Hughes looked on, baffled and bewildered.

'Ladies and gentlemen of the jury,' said Judge Roxburgh, after a few moments. 'I must unreservedly apologise to you – and to the witness – for that unfortunate incident.' He glared at Hughes. 'Such evidence has no place in my court. I intend to adjourn for the day, returning at 10 o'clock tomorrow morning. You may leave now, but I would like the two counsel to approach the bench.' The quietly sobbing Mrs Preece was led from the court by the policewoman.

Judge Roxburgh stood up as the clerk called: 'The court will rise.' The jury filed out and the public benches emptied. In the quiet courtroom, the two barristers stood nervously before the judge's bench.

'What was the meaning of that, Mr Hughes? The good lady was having difficulty enough understanding a scale plan of the crime scene without you introducing such distressing material. What earthly purpose, pray, was there in showing her a picture of a cadaver?'

'Your honour, my intention was merely to get the witness to confirm that it was she who discovered the victim's body behind the shed shown in the picture.'

'Quite apart from the fact that that information is recorded in the forensic report and in Detective Inspector Benjamin's deposition – both of which the jury have seen – it would have advanced the prosecution's case not one jot, if Mrs Preece had been able to identify the picture. Into the bargain you have distressed a very elderly lady.'

By courtroom 'rules of engagement', this was a severe reprimand, though Jeffrey Hughes seemed unfazed. 'But your honour...'.

Roxburgh lifted a pencil from his desk and pointed the end with the eraser at the unrepentant lawyer. 'But me no "buts", Mr Hughes!' After a long pause, he added: 'I will see you both at 10 o'clock tomorrow morning.' He turned and walked out.

Anthony's female guard in the dock stood and guided him towards the stairs leading down to the cell complex. He just had time to nod and smile at Tim Nugent on his way out.

There were only five passengers on the return journey and Anthony assumed that the Latvian shoplifter's bail application had been successful. Half-an-hour later, the van pulled into Carding's exercise yard and the prisoners wearily climbed out.

A despondent Herbert Parker appeared in Anthony's doorway ten minutes after his return. There was no sign of his book trolley, but he had a newspaper tucked under his arm.

'So how was your first day in court, my friend?' The old man leaned nonchalantly against the door frame.

'Well, I'm no expert in these matters, but I'd say we did quite well. And the old beak's a corker.'

Herbert gave a broad Caribbean grin. 'What did I tell you, man; what did I tell you?'

'What's more, the prosecuting counsel's a self-important prat. Grade One.'

Herbert became quite animated. 'Gets better and better! Always helps when the wankers are playin' for the opposition. If you get's my drift? And your brief? How did he perform?'

'It's a "she" actually.'

'My, my. We have a lady cricketer on the pitch at Shrewsbury, do we? She doin' alright?'

Anthony started to get the giggles, brought on by emotional fatigue. 'More than alright, mate. She's been knocking the opposition bowling all over the fucking park!' The cricketing badinage came to an abrupt halt, as Anthony's giggles turned to doleful tears. There was silence in the cell.

After a long pause, Herbert nervously shuffled in and sat beside Anthony on the bunk, placing a consoling arm around the younger man's shoulder. 'Glad you done well today, boss. Can't say mine's been a barrel of laughs.'

Anthony recalled the old self-imposed dictum he'd invented back in his days at public school, usually after a cruel beating with a plimsoll by one of the sadistic prefects. Five deep breaths, then positive thoughts.

'So what's up, Herbert? Had some bad news?'

The older man gazed down at his threadbare trainers. 'You could say that. Seems the lovely Vanessa's in Santo Domingo.'

'Where's that?'

'Dominican Republic. And there ain't no extradition treaty between the UK and Dominica. So Vanessa won't be getting' on a 747 back to Heathrow any time soon. Yours truly's gonna be facin' the music alone.' He paused and looked at the floor. 'Probably be my swan song.'

'When?'

'Malcolm in reception's boyfriend on North Wing reckons it might be as early as tomorrow.'

'Where? Shrewsbury?'

Herbert chuckled. 'Nah! Shrewsbury's just for shoplifters and murderers. I'll probably be comin' up at Manchester. They're sayin' the case will take a minimum of a week, so I'll be banged up in Strangeways every night. Which ain't what you'd call a five star hotel. Be leavin' before you in the morning, I guess. Think about me tomorrow?' He stood up and brushed his trousers straight.

'Of course I will, Herbert.'

He chucked his newspaper down on Anthony's bunk. It was the *Shropshire Star*. Beneath a banner headline reading "RED BUTTON MURDER TRIAL: DAY 1", was a picture of a man seated in a van, holding up one arm to shield his eyes. 'Fame at last, my friend,' the old man said with a laugh.

He turned in the doorway. 'Oh, and one last piece of advice, Anthony. It's communal shower time in half-an-hour. When the officer comes round, tell him you've got diarrhoea. Better still, just say "I've got the shits, sir."'

'Why's that?'

''cause there'll be a couple of real mean arse bandits in the shower rooms tonight. Wouldn't want to spoil your last night in prison, would you?'

Just before dawn, Anthony was awoken by a strange haunting sound. It was deep and rhythmical and regular, yet clearly not produced by anything mechanical. It was like a cross between a low base African tribal dirge and a Welsh male voice choir.

At first, its repeated drone was indecipherable, masked by the metallic drumming of objects being banged, in unison, against the steel cell doors all long the corridor.

But then, slowly, Anthony managed to decipher the mournful message: "Herbert's gone. Herbert's gone."

# XII

## *Verdict*

---

ANTHONY WAS RUDELY awoken at 7.00a.m. by the slamming open of his cell door. 'Crown Court van leaves in half-and-hour,' shouted a faceless guard. An enamel mug of tea had been left on the threshold.

The scene which greeted him twenty minutes later, as he stepped outside to board the prison van, was altogether different from 24 hours earlier. The prison's central courtyard was floodlit like a night-time football game.

The van was in place, its rear doors swung open, and the sanatorium's main gates had been rolled back. Four prisoners were climbing aboard. But also parked in the yard were two police cars, with their blue roof lights flashing, and an ambulance. A solemn-faced Ann Slocombe stood in attendance. Anthony moved towards the van.

After the prison van had slowly driven through Carding's entrance arch, a voice in the back of the dark interior said: 'Good man was Herbert. Salt of the earth.'

Barely realising he was contributing to the old trustee's encomium, Anthony murmured: 'Amen to that.' Then clasped his hands together and bent forward in prayer.

Half-an-hour later, the van slowly drove over the crown court's traffic flow plates, edged down the ramp and stopped. No Press photographers today. Nearly ten minutes elapsed before the prisoners were allowed to step down and file into the cell complex. Anthony was shown into the same cell and the door was slammed shut. He estimated that the court upstairs would be sitting in about forty minutes.

After a long wait, his cell door was finally thrust open, to reveal his young barrister, clutching an even larger pile of papers under her arm. She was already wearing her cravat and gown.

'Good morning, Anthony. Sleep well?'

'Up to a point, Lord Copper.' The Waugh reference was well received.

Clare Miller smiled. 'Same for me, I'm afraid. On a scale of nought-to-five, I'd rank the budget hotel I'm in at minus three!' She placed the court documents on the table and sat down.

'Right, let's get on, shall we; we've got a lot of ground to cover.' She removed her wristwatch and placed it between them on the table. 'We did well yesterday, Anthony, so let's build on that achievement. That blunder at the end of the afternoon by Jeff Hughes was a real bonus, wasn't it? Why are CPS briefs such berks? I don't suppose they'll be calling that cleaning lady back and I gather that their star witnesses hasn't shown up this morning.'

'Who's that?'

'An Italian button manufacturer.'

From the centre of the pile of papers, she slid out a single sheet, glancing at the top to confirm that it was the one she wanted.

'We're only calling three witnesses today: your gardener, your friend Terry Daniels and what may prove to be our key witness, a paper expert from Milton Keynes. Let's hope we don't get a "no show" too, because I'm relying on him to help us demolish the idea that your "Last night was wonderful" billet-doux was written this year.'

'What about me, Clare?'

She looked up and gave a mischievous smile. 'I'm sure you'll be pleased to hear that I've relieved you of that chore.'

She leant back in the chair. 'I'd like to take Terry Daniels last. Tell me, can he be trusted?'

'In what respect?'

'To speak the unvarnished truth. After all, you two spent an hour-and-a-half together that night in the hotel lounge, only five hours before Mrs Carlssen died. He's the closest thing we've got to an alibi.'

Anthony considered for a moment before replying. 'Yeah, Terry's OK – just so long as he leaves out all the Cockney repartee.'

'Bit of a joker, is he?'

'I'm afraid so.'

'Right, I'll watch out.'

'When do you suppose we might finish?'

'All being well, I'd hope we can be away from here by tea-time. I'm supposed to be in Derby tomorrow. And I imagine you'd rather not spend another night in Carding?'

'Not after last night.'

'Yes, I heard.'

There was a larger attendance for the court's second day, with five Press reporters on the bench to the right of the dock. Terry's ex-partner was once again dressed to the nines (this time her outfit even included a crimson fascinator). Noticeable new arrivals in the centre of the public benches were Walter and Doris Redknapp, looking as expectant as a couple of Andy Murray fans awaiting his appearance on Wimbledon's Centre Court. Behind them sat the portly bookbinder, Cyril Mumford. Barbara had yet to put in an appearance, though Tim Nugent sat talking animatedly to Stephenie.

For her second day in court, the Japanese lady juror was strikingly attired. She wore a midnight blue waisted suede jacket, over a dark blue satin polka-dot blouse, with her short black hair secured by a matching pleated headband. The other jurors' dresswear was as casual as on the first day.

Judge Roxburgh opened the proceedings without alluding to the incident of the previous afternoon. 'Mr Hughes, I believe your final witness has failed to arrive?'

'That is so, your honour. For which I apologise to the court. I had intended to call a technical representative of the old-established Italian button manufacturers Sangotti Frattelos of Langano. I am sorry to have to report that their representative, Signore Bendolo's flight yesterday was cancelled, due to industrial action at Milan Airport. Instead, therefore – with your permission – I should like to place before the court a two-page email which Signore Bendolo has sent. Exhibit 10.'

The judge nodded his ascent. 'Pray proceed, Mr Hughes.'

The clerk sprang up and began distributing copies to the jury. Of the two copies he handed Clare, she slid one through a gap in the dock's glass 'bars' for Anthony to read.

'Your honour: the first page - not in the best English, I fear - is by way of an introduction to the company: its history and professional reputation within the European clothing industry. The second, tabulated, page I shall attempt to summarise.

'In 2009, Sangottis were awarded a contract to supply red cuff buttons to an Italian clothing manufacturer that had secured an order to supply men's lightweight jackets to a British retail chain. Thirty thousand buttons were supplied; fourteen millimetres in diameter, all coloured red, predominantly made of resin and pigment. I would direct you to column 8 for their precise constitution.'

The barrister hesitated nervously, before pressing the video screens' button on his desk. 'The image on the left of the screen is a typical button from that 2009 order; the image on the right is the button previously presented in Detective Inspector Benjamin's evidence yesterday as Exhibit 4.' He pressed the switch again and the screens went black. Jeffrey Hughes craned his neck to adjust his cravat.

'So to all intents and purposes, members of the jury, the button found in Mrs Carlssen's clenched fist, exactly matches the remaining seven red buttons on the defendant's jacket. Unquestionably, the provenance of all eight buttons was Sangotti's factory in Langano. Of that there is no doubt, Thus, irrefutably confirming Anthony Metcalf's culpability in the death of Eva Carlssen.'

The barrister adjusted his wig and bent forward to sit down. But in a split second, Clare Miller was on her feet. 'I really must object, your honour. In the strongest possible terms.'

Wily old Roxburgh was ahead of her, but chose instead to let her deliver the *coup de grace*. He raised his eyebrows. 'The grounds for your objection, Miss Miller?'

'To bowdlerise the words of the American astronaut, the late Neil Armstrong, your honour: that was one small step from a table of button statistics to one huge assumption, on the part of my learned friend, of my client's guilt!'

The judge smiled at the concise analogy. 'I tend to agree, Miss Miller. Mr Hughes: I appreciate that you are somewhat 'at sea' down there, due to the absence of your expert witness. But I think we must stick with the facts as printed on the deposition and avoid making assumptions.' He then added tartly: 'Particularly as your witness has failed to put in an appearance. I shall direct the jury accordingly in my closing remarks.'

Hughes hung his head in mock-shame. 'I will be guided by your honour.'

'Miss Miller – do you wish to question the documents before the court?'

Clare decided to go for broke. She had already seen Hughes humiliated twice and she was banking on her paper expert's evidence. She really wanted to rub salt into this self-important barrister's wounds.

'Your honour, with my limited experience at the bar, I fear I am going to find it rather hard to cross-examine an Italian email. I have only one brief observation to make concerning the matter of the red button. With your permission, I would like to save that for my closing statement to the jury?'

It crossed the judge's mind (having once been a polished advocate himself) that the talented Miss Miller was probably "keeping her powder dry". If she did intend to demolish the Crown's case, what better moment to do so than at the end of her closing address. He nodded. 'As you wish, Miss Miller. Mr Hughes – does that conclude the prosecution's case?'

'It does, your honour,' replied Jeffrey Hughes, sheepishly.

'In that case, I think it would be an appropriate moment to adjourn and return in 20 minutes, when Miss Miller can open her case for the defence.'

'The court will rise.'

Both Clare and Anthony felt more relaxed after the break and the judge looked to be in good spirits. Jeffrey Hughes dejectedly flicked through some court papers. Though the game wasn't up, he felt it would now need to be a monumental blunder by the sure-footed Clare Miller to redress the balance in the Crown's favour.

The courtroom was silent, as the judge gave a paternal smile to the tall young woman barrister. 'Miss Miller?'

'Thank you, your honour. I should like to call as my first witness, Mr Robert Taylor of the wholesale paper manufacturers Dove Brothers of Milton Keynes.

After taking the oath in the witness box, Mr Taylor briefly explained to the court his technical background in the manufacturing of notepaper, greetings cards and other stationery.

'Have you had an opportunity to inspect the two items, known to the court as Exhibits 6 and 7 – one a blue envelope and the other a matching card?'

'I have, ma'am'.

'Then can you tell us, Mr Taylor: in your judgement, are the two items of the same age? Approximately.'

'No ma'am, most definitely not.'

The video screens blinked into life.

'For the benefit of the jury, your honour, Exhibit 6 on the left, is the hand-addressed envelope, bearing a franked first class stamp which shows that it was posted in Ludlow on 18th August 2015. On the right-hand side of the screen is a hand-written card, initialled "A".

She turned to Robert Taylor.'So, which is the older?'

'Exhibit 7, by a long way, ma'am.'

'Would you care to postulate for us how long "a long way" might be?'

Taylor stroked his chin. 'From our microscopic examination of the card's fibres, I'd say it is five or six years old.'

'While Exhibit 6?'

'Much easier to date. Almost certainly manufactured this year.'

'Thank you, Mr Taylor.' Clare gave a sideways glance at her neighbour and sat down.

Jeffrey Hughes' cross-examination of the paper expert was plodding and perfunctory and he was unable to dent the witness's central assertion that the card and the envelope were of different ages.

Next into the witness box was Mike Green, the Metcalf's gardener. Standing bolt upright in an immaculate grey suit, he told the court about the mysterious disappearance of the can of weed killer from the unlocked garage at Kynaston Barn. His evidence went unchallenged.

Through some ingenious procedural devices, Clare Miller neatly paced her performance so that Terry Daniels would be the last witness before the lunch recess.

Though the market trader's initial demeanour had something of an over-confident swagger, she soon brought him to heel. She moved subtly from the saga of the ancient Bradshaw railway timetable to his evening drink with Anthony in The Feathers Hotel.

'And how would you describe Mr Metcalf's mood on that evening, Mr Daniels?'

'Not too chipper.'

'By that, I take it you mean "subdued"?'

'Yes.'

'Did he bring up the matter of a holiday abroad?'

'Yes, ma'am. To the Canaries.'

'He had received a proposition from Mrs Carlssen, I believe?'

'Yes. ma'am.'

'And what was his reaction to the idea?'

'He said he thought it was a crazy idea and that he'd told her he didn't want to know about it. I believe the word he used was "crackpot".'

'And then?'

'And then he started going on about opera.'

The judge leaned forward across his desk to better hear the market trader's evidence. 'Miss Miller, did the witness say "opera"?'

'I believe so, your honour. Mr Daniels, for the befit of the jury can you explain how the conversation that evening jumped from the subject of holidays in the Canary Islands to opera?'

Terry Daniels was momentarily floored, but quickly recovered. 'Well, as I recall, I think I'd referred to Mrs Carlssen as being a "merry widow", or some such phrase, 'cause of all the 'usbands she'd 'ad. And Mr Metcalf corrected me and said "no" she wasn't like the character in the operetta by... I can't remember the composer's name...'

'Lehár. Franz Lehár,' murmured the judge, with a smile.

'That's the fellow, your honour!' Terry nodded thanks at Roxburgh. 'Ant said she – Mrs Carlssen, that is – was more like a character from one of Puccini's operas.'

'Did he cite any?'

'Well, ma'am, I'm a bit out of my depth here, so to speak, being as I'm not a great opera fan. Dusty Springfield and Tom Jones are more my sort of music.'

Jeffrey Hughes rose languidly to his feet. 'Your honour – time is pressing on, and whilst it is illuminating to know of my learned friend's knowledge of opera, I really fail to see what it has to do with the case before the court.'

'Patience is a virtue, Mr Hughes. I'm quite sure Miss Miller is not leading us up the garden path.' He nodded down at the young barrister. 'Pray continue.'

'Thank you, your honour. No, there'll be no horticultural peregrinations, I assure you.' She turned to face Terry Daniels again. The operas of Giacomo Puccini, you say, Mr Daniels?'

During the brief interruption, Terry had flashed a quick look across to his friend in the dock. He was determined to help him and had now marshalled his recollections thoroughly. His next answer was like a quote from *The New Grove Dictionary of Music*.

'Yes, ma'am. We began with Mimi from *La Bohème*. Then Ant – err Mr Metcalf - referred to the diva in *Tosca*. But the last example was way over my head, I'm afraid.'

'And who was that?'

'The principal character in *Madame Butterfly*. He said her name, but I can't remember it.'

'Cio-Cio-san?'

'That's her. He said Mrs Carlssen was just like her.'

Clare left a long pause. She wanted every member of the jury to hear Terry's next answer. 'Did Mr Metcalf say why?'

'He just said it would suit him well if Mrs Carlssen was to go the same way.' He shrugged. 'That's all.'

'Your honour, with your permission, may I briefly summarise for members of the jury unfamiliar with this particular opera, the plot of *Madame Butterfly*?'

Judge Roxburgh lounged back in his high-backed chair. "This is going to be good" he thought to himself. 'By all means, Miss Miller.' Jeffrey Hughes scowled.

'Cio-Cio-san, AKA Madame Butterfly, members of the jury, is a poor Japanese concubine trapped in an arranged marriage with an American naval officer named Pinkerton. One day, Lieutenant Pinkerton informs her that he is returning to the United States, to resume his conventional marriage, leaving her behind in Nagasaki. She is utterly devastated. In the opera's final act, Cio-Cio-san comes onto the stage carrying a samurai warrior's sword, and ritually disembowels herself in front of the audience.'

Across the courtroom, there was the same delayed reaction of disbelief as there had been the day before, to the vision of the white hand of the corpse. Then uproar.

The Japanese lady juror screeched out in horror and then slumped forward. Journalists wrote furiously, while ushers looked earnestly towards the bench for direction. Jeffrey Hughes banged his expensive ballpoint pen on the desk, shattering its case. Clare Miller (having just hit a six over the sight screens) remained serenely calm.

After several minutes the hubbub subsided and Judge Roxburgh was able to adjourn the court for lunch, with the Japanese lady being escorted to the jury room by a young woman colleague. Terry crossed the court floor to greet Tina, Tim and Stephenie left to find a sandwich shop, while Judge Roxburgh retired for a solitary lunch in his chambers.

At 2.00p.m. sharp the clerk to the court was poised to knock on the door of the jury room, ready to re-admit the jury. But a hand gesture from the judge made him hesitate. 'Would counsel kindly approach the bench?' he asked the two barristers. He was studying a small piece of paper.

In a low voice, he told them: 'During the recess, I received this note from the jury foreman, in which he seeks my permission to stand down the Japanese lady jury member. It seems she has been sobbing inconsolably throughout the lunch break, to such an extent that it is now beginning to distress some of her fellow jury members. We need to restore an air of calm dignity to these proceedings. Obviously it must be my decision, but I should like to have both your views. Mr Hughes?'

After two reprimands, Jeffrey Hughes was certainly not going to fall foul of this pre-eminent circuit judge for a third time. 'I have no objection, your honour.'

'Miss Miller?'

'With great respect, your honour, this lady is not unwell, she is merely distressed by some of this morning's evidence. Significant evidence, which the court was entitled to hear. We all come here – counsel, jurors and, of course, your honour – to see justice done. I would respectfully submit, that unless the lady is judged to be medically unfit to return, she has a duty to the court to remain on the jury.'

'Very well Mr Hughes, Miss Miller, give me a few moments and I will send a note back to the foreman. Then we will resume.'

Shortly afterwards, a hand-written note was passed to the clerk, who delivered it to the jury room. Two minutes later he opened the door to re-admit all twelve members of the jury. He closed the two small doors of the jury box shut with a resounding bang, as if sounding the overture to the final act.

Jeffrey Hughes rose to cross-examine Terry Daniels, now looking relaxed and pleased with his defence of his friend Anthony.

The barrister glanced down at his desk, as if consulting an important document. 'Mr Daniels, how would you describe the nature of your friendship with the defendant?'

Terry shrugged. 'I don't know, really. We're just good muckers, as you might say.'

'In English?'

'Pardon?'

'Could you re-phrase your answer into the Queen's English, for the benefit of the jury?'

'We're good pals. How's that?'

'Thank you, Mr Daniels. Apart from your allusion to the operetta *The Merry Widow* – which we heard about before the adjournment – did you make any other observations that evening about the late Mrs Carlssen?'

Terry knew very well what he would answer, but like a seasoned music hall comedian, he was aware that timing was of the essence. After a long pause, he said: 'I told him I thought she had nice gams.'

'"Gams" being cockney argot for legs, I believe?' asked Hughes.

Terry looked at the judge. 'No. I think the origin of the word is from the Italian "gamba."' Roxburgh nodded.

The prosecution barrister paused, visibly irritated. 'And what was his reaction?'

Terry pursed his lips and frowned. 'Sorry, I don't recall. I rather think he said: "I'll just have another half of lager, Terry."' Several jurors tittered at this exchange.

Hughes adjusted his wig, sensing that he was up against a solid – and loyal – brick wall. 'No further questions, your honour.'

There was a general murmur along the Press bench. Fresh pages of notebooks were turned as Jeffrey Hughes – still on his feet – prepared to begin his closing address.

'Your honour, members of the jury. I need not detain you long, since ample evidence has been put before you over the last two days, to show that the defendant, Anthony Ellington Metcalf, took the life of Mrs Eva Carlssen in an act of cold-blooded revenge, for her several misguided acts of importuning. Acts which she clearly intended would re-start a former sexual liaison.

'Her final gesture – which most would view as an act of extreme generosity – was to make arrangements to take the defendant on holiday to the Canary Islands. She had even purchased the flight tickets and made a reservation at a luxury hotel in Las Palmas in their two names.

'But it was this act of generosity which drove the accused over the edge. Armed with a lethal quantity on the strongest poison available on the market - taken from his own garage - he visited her late at night and forcibly poisoned her. It must have been a horribly brutal act, as the evidence in the cottage showed that she put up fierce resistance. As she was expiring, he callously dragged her outside and dumped her body in the garden.' The Japanese lady sobbed quietly in the back corner of the jury box.

'Undoubtedly, the most incriminating of the evidence which has been placed before you is the red cuff button found in the deceased's hand.' Several jurors looked towards the blank video screen at the end of the jury box, believing the barrister was about to show them more lurid images. But he wasn't. Hughes sat down, feeling pleased with himself. He straightened his cravat.

Jurors and journalists looked expectantly towards the young woman barrister as she stood up.

'Miss Miller?'

'Your honour, members of the jury. Would that life was as cut-and-dried as my learned friend here has tried to suggest. Possibly such torrid melodramas are enacted in some television soap operas, but not in 21st century rural Shropshire.

'All the character evidence concerning my client which has been placed before the court, has been of an exemplary nature. Happily married and the proprietor of a well-respected Ludlow bookshop, Anthony Metcalf suddenly finds himself the victim of a sexual predator. A female stalker, no less: Mrs Eva Carlssen, neé Perrier, neé Bertorelli. A woman with a seemingly bottomless purse. Owner of a classic German sports racing car, worth £2-million, used as a mere run-about. Mr Daniels' "merry widow" observation was shrewd indeed. But, like Lehár's heroine, Mrs Carlssen quickly discovered that all her riches couldn't buy the object of her lustful desire – Anthony Metcalf.

'Not one shred of evidence – from restaurant table tittle-tattle to the absence of tell-tale gravel chippings or any sign of his fingerprints (save on the can of weed killer, which had been taken from his own garage) in the holiday cottage – has been produced by the prosecution to show that the defendant succumbed to the lady's blandishments. Ever. Not once. Her ultimate gesture - to spirit him off to the Canary Islands - he described as "crackpot".'

Clare stared at the Japanese lady, once again sobbing quietly. The arm of a neighbouring woman juror had been placed around her shoulder. Judge Roxburgh glanced across at the box, but decided to let this impressive young advocate keep the floor. He nodded to Clare to continue.

'I now come to the most perplexing piece of evidence put before the court – namely the blue card in the blue envelope. We know that the envelope was posted in Ludlow on 18th August this year. In his evidence, the paper expert Mr Taylor told this court, in emphatic terms, that the date of manufacture of the card it contained is six years earlier. So is it not more likely that Mrs Carlssen had retained the notelet (the "Last night was wonderful" message), as a fond and treasured memento of their former liaison, in 2009? Women have been known - and I confess to being one of them - to retain strange romantic keepsakes: a pebble from a beach, or a dried flower, pressed in a holiday novel.

'And Detective Inspector Benjamin's second interview with Mr Metcalf placed him firmly at home with his wife on the night before the blue envelope was posted. Why on earth would he send Mrs Carlssen such a contradictory message?'

'Now I shall deal with the red button.' Clare Miller put down the sheaf of papers she had been holding. Her final flourish would be extemporary.

'"Beyond reasonable doubt", ladies and gentlemen, is a phrase which you have heard used several times in this courtroom. In the case of Regina versus Metcalf it must be your watchword. It is one of the tenets of English law.

'The defence does not dispute the fact that the buttons on Mr Metcalf's jacket and the button found in the deceased's hand are of the same provenance.' She paused to note the jury's surprised reaction to this admission. 'But so too are the cuff buttons of 3,749 other British jackets. None of which the police have inspected.

'No fragment of cotton thread or jacket cloth material has been detected that would link Exhibit 4 to Exhibit 10. So can you, in all honesty – beyond reasonable doubt - be certain that the button found in Mrs Carlssen's hand came from my client's jacket? I think not.'

Clare collected up her brief, ready to conclude. 'Your Honour – may I close by alluding to the short story by Sir Arthur Conan Doyle, entitled *Silver Blaze*? This is sometimes known by the more popular sobriquet of "The curious incident of the dog in the night-time." In essence, the story's moral is: "Never substitute supposition for absence of evidence". Thank you, your honour.'

The judge gave Clare a knowing smile. Lehár, Puccini and now the great detective himself, were more than he'd bargained for when he came to Shrewsbury. 'I think that would be an appropriate moment for us to adjourn. When we return, I will address the jury.'

'The court will rise.'

Stephenie and Barbara were sitting on a bench in the sunshine, in front of Shrewsbury's Shire Hall, which stands alongside the crown court complex. Tim Nugent had offered to stand guard in the court lobby, ready to alert the two women of the resumption.

Towering above them was a lofty stone monument, taller even than Nelson's column in Trafalgar Square. It was surmounted by a stone effigy of a military figure. A notice at the base of the column identified it as Lord Rowland Hill (1772-1842). Tim came and stood behind the two women.

Gazing upwards from behind her designer sunglasses, Stephenie asked the young man: 'Who's that perched up there, Tim?'

'Lord Rowland Hill, known to all the troops who served under him as "Daddy Hill", because of the civilised way he always treated them. Friend and trusted confidante of the Iron Duke, he guarded the General's right flank at the Battle of Waterloo. He even led the penultimate charge, which routed the French. Generally regarded by historians to be the greatest military strategist who ever lived. The court is about to resume, so shall we go in?'

On the resumption, the Press benches were full and the spectators in the public gallery had risen to double figures. Detectives Benjamin and Tierney were seated in the front row. The Japanese juror sat calmly in her back bench position. The court rose as Judge William Roxburgh entered from behind his marble screen for the penultimate time.

'Firstly, I wish to reiterate to all the members of the jury, my apology of yesterday afternoon for the distressing image which you briefly had to witness.

'Secondly, I wish to express my sincere admiration to those of you who may have found parts of these proceedings upsetting. This is a court of law, ladies and gentlemen. And law – the correct administration of that law – can sometimes be harsh.' The Japanese lady blushed.

'Briefly I must address my next remarks to the members of the Press. You are to disregard and not report any matters concerning the defendant's period of employment as a schoolmaster in Sussex. I rule that they were within the law then obtaining, and are protected under a legally-enforceable confidentiality agreement.

'Concerning the prosecution's closing remarks in the matter of the red cuff button, you may safely conclude that the button found in the victim's hand did, in fact, come from the Italian manufacturer Sangotti Fratellos. But no more than that.'

He turned back towards the jury. 'But now it is up to you. Twelve good men – and women – and true, to reach your verdict on the single charge of murder, brought against the defendant, Anthony Ellington Metcalf. And if you are unable to reach a unanimous verdict by the end of this afternoon, I will accept a majority verdict, either of 11:1 or 10:2. If you need further time for your deliberations beyond 5.00p.m., I may ask you to return tomorrow.

'In her eloquent closing statement, counsel for the defence made reference to a work by Sir Arthur Conan Doyle. Even those of you on the jury who are unfamiliar with that writer's huge oeuvre, will surely be aware that, first and last, Mr Sherlock Holmes was a scrupulous observer of fair play. So it is with the case before you today. You must be certain, beyond reasonable doubt, that your verdict is based solely and exclusively on fair play. Neither nuance, oblique suspicion nor smutty innuendo should play any part in your deliberations.'

Roxburgh paused and looked, not at the jury, but directly – piercingly – into Anthony's eyes. 'In essence, you are being asked to decide whether Anthony Metcalf murdered Eva Carlssen.' He leaned back in his chair and nodded to the clerk.

'The court will rise.'

Stephenie and Barbara were sitting disconsolately on the bench beneath the Hill monument. The jury had been out for almost two hours and they were both resigned to having to drive back up in the morning.

'What do you reckon,' Barbara asked, 'Is this a good sign or a bad sign?'

'Search me, darling. Oscars and BAFTAs are my *forte*. And their juries usually take three months to make up their minds!'

'Do you want to stay over at our place tonight?'

'Well if it does go over into tomorrow, I was thinking I might try and find a quiet little wayside inn for the night. You see, I've offered to give Tim a lift back, as he came up on the train.'

Barbara did a full thespian double-take. 'Steph! That boy's young enough to be your grandson!' she snapped.

Her friend shrugged her padded shoulders. 'What's wrong with that? Wasn't it Katharine Hepburn who said: "If you observe all the rules, you'll miss all the fun"?'

Tim appeared and placed a hand lightly on Stephenie's shoulder. 'Court's resuming.'

Once the jurors were all seated in their places on the two benches, the foreman rose, holding a slip of paper.

'Are you agreed on your verdict?'

'We are, your honour.'

'And is that the verdict of you all?'

'It is, your honour. We find the defendant not guilty of the charge.'

A huge wave of delighted relief swept through the court. Journalists pocketed their notebooks and rushed outside, while the public in the rear gallery stood up, many smiling. One or two hugged each other. Stephenie burst into tears, to be consoled by Tim, with a stony-faced Barbara looking on. Apart from a sullen Jeffrey Hughes, dejectedly packing his briefcase, the only other person in the courtroom who seemed shocked by the verdict was a crestfallen Doris Redknapp.

Anthony slumped forward in his chair, his head touching his knees. Above the hubbub, he heard the familiar clank of a keychain and of a door being unlocked. A hand rested lightly on his shoulder. He looked sideways at the opened door at the back of the dock.

'You're free to go, sir.'

Stepping from the dock, he followed Barbara and Stephenie out into the fresh air. And freedom.

Tim Nugent was standing by the bench beneath the Hill monument. Anthony and Tim shook hands. On the seat was a cardboard box. 'The Carding prison reception sent this over for you on the van this afternoon,' he told Anthony.

Anthony flipped the box's corrugated flaps open, revealing his clothes and personal belongings. On the top of the pile was a well-worn copy of A. E. Houseman's *A Shropshire Lad*, with a yellow Post-It sticker emerging from the middle.

Standing exultantly in the evening sunshine, Anthony read the hand-written dedication on the flyleaf.

> *To Anthony:*
> *Now you have your well-deserved freedom.*
> *I too am free and won't have to spend the*
> *rest of my days banged up for a crime I*
> *didn't commit.*
> > *Sincerely, Herbert*

Anthony flipped through the pages to the fluorescent yellow bookmark.

> *They hang us now in Shrewsbury jail:*
> *The whistles blow forlorn.*
> *And trains all night groan on the rail*
> *To men that die at dawn.*

- E N D -

# Nick Jones

... has spent his life connected with buildings. Initially working as a surveying assistant on a major tunnelling project under the City of London, he moved into architectural journalism, working for a publishing group which was part of Express Newspapers. He first edited specialist supplements for the weekly newspaper Building Design then later became Editor of the conservation monthly Building Refurbishment. He has contributed to many other architectural publications. His debut novel 'King's Cross' was published in August 2015. The writer now lives in Herefordshire. Contact the author at www.ampersandworld.co.uk